"Don't cry."

"Why not?" Rebecca asked bitterly.

"Because if you cry I'll have to comfort you, and one thing can lead to another...."

He sounded kind and caring, and, knowing that Jason didn't care a fig about her, she was pathetically grateful that someone did.

As his face swam in and out of focus, she caught hold of his hand. "Thank you."

"Good night and sweet dreams." He rose to his feet.

Still clinging to his hand, she begged hoarsely, "Don't leave me. Please don't leave me. I don't want to be on my own tonight...."

LEE WILKINSON lives with her husband in a three-hundred-year-old stone cottage in an English village, which most winters gets cut off by snow. They both enjoy traveling, and recently, joining forces with their daughter and son-in-law, spent a year going around the world "on a shoestring" while their son looked after Kelly, their much-loved German shepherd dog. Lee's hobbies are reading and gardening and holding impromptu barbecues for her long-suffering family and friends.

ONE NIGHT WITH THE TYCOON

LEE WILKINSON

THE MILLIONAIRE AFFAIR

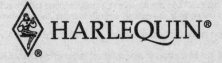

TORONTO • NEW YORK • LONDON
AMSTERDAM • PARIS • SYDNEY • HAMBURG
STOCKHOLM • ATHENS • TOKYO • MILAN • MADRID
PRAGUE • WARSAW • BUDAPEST • AUCKLAND

ISBN 0-373-82025-9

ONE NIGHT WITH THE TYCOON

First North American Publication 2005.

Copyright © 2004 by Lee Wilkinson.

CHAPTER ONE

HER smile as sparkling as a tiara and her heart as heavy as lead, Rebecca Ferris stood in attendance while her eighteen-year-old stepsister married the only man she had ever loved.

Holding the bride's bouquet, she waited while Lisa and the Honourable Jason Beaumont, newly pronounced man and wife, kissed each other. Then, stiff as any robot, she followed them and the rest of the wedding party, into the vestry for the register to be signed.

After an unusually cold, wet start to the summer, the long-range forecast for mid-July had predicted a warm, dry spell, and the wedding day had been set for the sixteenth.

Helen, the bride's mother, had arranged for a late ceremony and an evening reception. As the weather was holding wonderfully the photographs were taken outside Elmslee's old grey church, with a backdrop of ancient yew trees.

Guests stood around in little groups in the early-evening sunshine, discussing what a handsome pair the newlyweds made—the bride, blonde, petite and beautiful, and the slimly built groom, tall, fair and with matinée-idol looks.

When the photographer was finally satisfied, ribbons fluttering on the white wedding cars, they were driven through the picturesque village and back to Elmslee Manor, the Ferrises' family home for more than three centuries.

Lisa, who as a very small child had come with her mother to live at Elmslee, had been impatient to get away. Much preferring the bright lights of nearby London, she had moved into Jason's Knightsbridge flat at the very first opportunity.

Rebecca had been born at Elmslee. She loved the small

Elizabethan manor, with its mullioned windows and barley-sugar chimneys, and had missed it sadly when she left.

Now it was to be sold. Helen had put Elmslee on the market and was planning to take a flat in London to be near her newly married daughter.

Knowing how much her father would have hated the idea, Rebecca had ventured to protest.

Her stepmother had said sharply that, money aside, now Lisa had gone, the ten-bedroomed manor was much too big for her, and far too quiet.

Today, however, Elmslee was anything but quiet. The house and gardens were *en fête*.

A large marquee had been set up on the south-west side of the house, with its smooth lawns and dark cedars. There were space-heaters on the terrace, just in case it turned cool, and a lively orchestra ready for the evening's festivities.

A paved area in front of the old orangery was to be used as an extra car park, floodlights were in place in the grounds, and coloured lanterns had been strung between the trees.

The second Mrs Ferris, well-used—after sixteen years—to playing her part as lady of the manor, had excelled herself. All the arrangements for the reception had been put into place with astonishing speed and efficiency.

Before Jason had time to change his mind again, one of the aunts had observed cattily.

In a hall beautifully decorated with huge swags of flowers, the wedding party lined up to greet the guests as they filed in.

It was an ordeal Rebecca had been dreading but, head held high, she was managing to smile her way through it when Great-Aunt Letty was announced, and began to move down the line.

After presenting her leathery cheek for a kiss, the old lady grumbled, 'I don't know why the ceremony had to be so late. Fashion, I dare say. It'll be nearly my bedtime before we get to eat.'

Then in a piercing whisper, 'I was most surprised when I got a wedding invitation with Lisa's name on it. I understood that *you* were engaged to young what's-his-name…'

Rebecca swallowed hard. 'Well, yes, I was, but—'

'What on earth were you thinking of, letting that spoilt brat of a stepsister steal him from you?'

Seeing the stricken look on her great-niece's face, Letty patted her hand consolingly. 'Never mind, love. Take it from me, there's as good fish in the sea as ever came out of it. You might even say better.'

Letty moved on, and, lifting her chin, Rebecca continued to smile and shake hands with people she scarcely knew. Then thankfully the last guest was announced, one that she recognised as being her stepmother's special crony.

During a sudden lull in the general noise level, she heard Helen say clearly, 'Of course, poor Rebecca's terribly disappointed. But really there was no point in trying to cling to a man who's never really wanted her. So humiliating…'

Well-aware that everyone within earshot was listening avidly, as a couple of waiters began to circulate with trays of champagne, Rebecca slipped away and escaped through a side-door.

Half blinded by a combination of low sun and tears she was struggling not to let fall, she hurried down the garden, her ankle-length, lilac-coloured dress brushing the clumps of summer flowers that edged the paved path.

Stumbling a little in her haste, she skirted the marquee and made her way past the shrubbery to the old, circular summer house that stood on a little knoll. Disused for a long time, the place had been neglected in recent years, and even more so since her father's death.

Climbing the steps, she pushed open the creaking door of what, as a child, had always been her sanctuary when she was feeling unhappy or misunderstood, and sank onto the wooden bench that ran around the walls.

After several days of sunshine the musty air was quite

warm, and it was blessedly dark, the grimy windows covered on the inside by spiders' webs, and the outside by rampaging ivy.

While Lisa had flitted from boyfriend to boyfriend since the age of fifteen, Jason was the only man Rebecca had ever wanted, and for the first time since losing him she lowered her guard and let the bitter tears run down her cheeks unchecked.

Suddenly the creak of the door opening made her look up sharply. A bright shaft of low sunlight slanted in, dazzling her. All she could make out was a tall, dark shape filling the doorway.

'I've been told that women always cry at weddings, but don't you think this is overdoing it a bit?' a male voice asked drily.

Mortified, she shielded her face with her hand.

He closed the door with his heel, and set his back to it.

'I'd like to be alone,' she informed him thickly.

Mockingly, he said, 'You sound like Greta Garbo.'

'Go away! Please go away,' she begged.

After a moment, hearing no further sound of movement, she glanced up.

Leaning nonchalantly against the door, he was holding a bottle of champagne by the neck, and two long-stemmed flutes.

She couldn't see his face clearly in the gloom, but his hair was very dark and his teeth very white as he smiled at her.

'What do you want?' she demanded.

'I'm here to offer my condolences.'

Though his words *might* have been described as sympathetic, his tone certainly couldn't.

She wasn't sorry. The last thing she wanted was to be pitied by a perfect stranger.

Though he obviously knew who she was.

'Who are you?' she demanded.

There was the slightest pause, before he told her, 'My name's Graydon Gallagher.' Getting no reaction, he added casually, 'Most of my friends call me Gray.'

Coming over to sit by her side, he looked at her carefully in the half-light.

Her ash-brown hair was taken up into a chignon and adorned with a circlet of fresh flowers. Around her neck, which was long and slender, she was wearing a single string of pearls.

Despite the careful make-up her heart-shaped face looked pale and drawn, her wide-set almond eyes were brimming with tears, and mauve shadows beneath them suggested that she hadn't slept properly for weeks.

In most of the photographs he had seen of her, her face had been serene, her amber-coloured eyes clear, her mouth wide and full, but with hardly any bow at all, looking as if she might smile at any moment.

Though it was not beautiful in the conventional sense, he had found it a fascinating face, full of character, and had thought cynically that Jason's taste was improving enormously.

A lot of the females he had got entangled with in the past had been glamorous gold-diggers, out for all they could get, with beauty their only asset.

This woman, Gray had felt sure, was different. She had brains and—he would have bet any amount of money—strength and resilience.

Though she could be—and considering the family's circumstances, probably *was*—after Jason's money, she looked the sort that might make that feckless young man a good wife.

In the event she had been pipped at the post by her young stepsister, and was obviously not relishing it.

As he studied her she sniffed, and wiped away a tear that was trickling down her chin.

With a twisted smile at the triteness of it, he felt in his pocket with his free hand and passed her a folded hankie.

'Thank you.' She blew her nose and scrubbed at her wet cheeks. 'Are you a friend of Jason's?'

'I've known him all his life. For a time we lived in the same London square, only a few houses apart.'

'And you've stayed close?'

'Yes, you could say that.'

During the weeks that she and Jason had been engaged, he had jealously wanted her all to himself.

Not particularly gregarious, and head over heels in love, she had been pleased by this show of male possessiveness. But because he had neglected his usual social circle, she hadn't met all that many of his friends.

His voice ironic, Gray pursued, 'I had thought that when he got married he might ask me to be his best man, but...' Broad shoulders lifted in a shrug.

Thinking back, she remarked, 'I didn't see you amongst the guests.'

'Unfortunately my plane was delayed on take-off at JFK, so not only did I miss the actual service, but I was also rather late arriving at the house.'

Frowning, she said, 'So you weren't announced?'

'No. After parking my car, I came in by the rear entrance. I was just about to join the merry throng when I happened to overhear your stepmother's rather unkind remarks.'

'Oh.' She flushed hotly.

'I noticed you slip away.'

'And you followed me? Why?'

'You looked so unhappy that I thought a drop of vintage champagne might help to alleviate your—er—disappointment.'

At close quarters she could just make out that his face was lean and attractive, with a strong chin and a fine straight nose. He must be in his late twenties or early thirties, she guessed. Though his eyes gleamed brilliantly beneath dark brows, she couldn't tell whether they were grey or light blue.

He set the glasses on the bench and, his movements deft, began to open the bottle, observing gravely, 'Remarkable restorative powers, champagne.'

Stripping off the foil, he untwisted the wire, and used his thumb to gently ease out the cork. 'Transporting it may have made it a little lively. However, I'm sure we'll cope.'

'Thank you, but I really don't want any champagne.'

'Now, is that nice?' he demanded plaintively, as the cork came out with a loud pop and ricocheted off the wooden ceiling. Pouring the foaming wine, he added, 'To save wounding my feelings you could at least *pretend* to be grateful.'

'I am, of course. But I—'

'You don't look a bit grateful,' he objected, peering at her closely.

Becoming convinced that he was just having a bit of cruel fun at her expense, she said raggedly, 'I'd be *very* grateful if you'd just go away.'

'I'll think about it when you've had at least one glass of champagne,' he promised.

'I don't *want* a glass of champagne…any more than I want your company.'

'You may not *want* my company, but I'm convinced you *need* it.'

'Why should I need it?'

'To bolster your ego. It must be quite deflating to be ditched for one's stepsister. Though I gather you all stayed friends, as you're the chief bridesmaid?'

When she said nothing, he observed with mock sympathy, 'It can't be easy being a bridesmaid when everyone knows you should have been the bride.'

In truth it was the hardest thing she had ever done. Only her pride, allied to a lifetime of concealing her feelings, had made it possible.

It was that same fierce pride that had allowed them all to 'stay friends'. Determined that no one, least of all Lisa and Jason, should know just how devastated she was, she had struggled to hide her anguish behind a façade of calm acceptance.

'However,' her companion was continuing blandly, 'I do think you should make an effort to put in an appearance at the reception.'

Her hands balled into fists. 'After what Helen said, I can't…I just can't!'

'So what *do* you plan to do? You won't be able to hide out here indefinitely. The minute the sun goes down it'll start to get chilly, and, while the marquee appears to be heated, this place certainly isn't.'

'As soon as everyone's eating, I'll slip back to the house.'

He clicked his tongue reprovingly and asked, 'How can the evening's festivities—which must, incidentally, have cost your stepmother a bomb—go with a bang when the chief bridesmaid will be hiding in her room indulging in tears of jealous rage?'

Her hand itched to smack his good-looking face.

Barely managing to repress this sudden, quite untypical urge to violence, she said curtly, 'I'll be doing no such thing.'

'You can hardly deny that you're hiding now.'

Watching her bite her lip, he went on, 'You should be out there celebrating with them. While the occasion may not be quite as joyful as you'd hoped, at least, between you, you've managed to keep Jason in the family.

'No small triumph. Quite a lot of other women have tried and failed.'

Handing her a glass of champagne with such calm assurance that she automatically took it, Gray suggested, 'But in the circumstances, instead of toasting your stepsister's success, what if we just drink to the future?'

At that precise moment, her future looked cold and bleak and empty.

When she made no move, he raised a level brow. 'Or perhaps that doesn't appeal to you?'

'No, it doesn't.'

'Why not?' he challenged. 'Though you may have lost one prospective husband, you've plenty of time to find another. You're still quite young. Twenty-one? Twenty-two?'

'I'm twenty-three,' she said, and instantly regretted telling him.

'Five years older than the blushing bride! Dear me, no wonder you're absolutely furious. With all that extra experience you should have been able to hold on to your man.

'Though in all fairness, I must say that where Jason is concerned it might not have been easy.

'He's always had a roving eye, and because of his wealthy background and his title, not to mention his looks, he's had more women chasing after him than you could shake a stick at.'

The 'roving eye' stung, and, her voice trembling with rage, she cried, 'You're absolutely hateful!'

Looking completely unmoved, Gray said, 'But don't despair. Though you may not be a raving beauty like your stepsister, as far as I can see in this light you're still very attractive—'

'Thanks,' she said glacially.

'So you surely must have plenty going for you.'

'Funny how I can't think of a single thing.' The bitterness came through.

'Then let's drink to one another, and a change of fortune.' He raised his glass. 'Here's to us, and whatever makes us happy.'

Feeling goaded and driven, with an unaccustomed recklessness, she took an incautious gulp of the fizzy champagne and promptly choked.

As she coughed and spluttered, he patted her back solicitously, enquiring at length, 'That better?'

Unable to speak, she nodded.

'Why don't you try another drink?' he urged.

This time she was a great deal more careful, and after a couple of sips managed a husky, 'Thank you.'

'Is that genuine gratitude, or just good manners?' he enquired quizzically.

'Good manners,' she flashed back. 'As I said earlier, if it's genuine gratitude you want, you'll go away and leave me alone.'

'So you can start crying again?'

'I'll cry if I want to,' she retorted. Then groaned inwardly, aware that she had sounded childish.

'I suppose I can't blame you,' he said magnanimously, 'hurt pride can be the very devil. And the fact that your chance to marry into money has been snatched away must be galling.'

'Money has absolutely nothing to do with it. I loved him.'

'Past tense?'

'No, I still love him.'

Gray frowned. 'You sound as if you mean it.'

'I *do* mean it.' She took another drink. 'He was the only man I've ever loved, and I thought he loved me.' But it seemed she'd been wrong.

At the best of times champagne tended to make her a little tipsy. Now, not having eaten all day, it was going straight to her head, and making her feel light and floaty.

But at least that was better than the leaden weight of misery that had weighed her down since she had discovered Jason's and Lisa's perfidy.

Replenishing her glass, Gray suggested, 'Suppose you tell me all about it?'

Used to hiding her emotions—even from her family and friends—she had no intention of opening her heart to this rude and abrasive stranger.

Reading her expression, he said coaxingly, 'Go on, you may as well. It'll do you the world of good to get it off your chest.'

She half shook her head.

'At the very least it'll help to pass the time. Start by telling me how you and Jason met.'

Already the champagne was loosening her tongue, and without meaning to she found herself saying, 'We met at work.'

Responding to his undoubted interest, she continued, 'My father died at the beginning of last year. After his death, Bowman Ferris, the finance company his great-grandfather had helped to found in the early nineteen-hundreds, was bought out by Finance International.

'PLFI, as it's widely known, is an Anglo-American banking corporation owned by Philip Lorne, Jason's uncle, and Jason was brought in as the new MD of the London branch.

'A few months later when Miss Swensen, his American PA, asked to be transferred back to the States to be closer to her terminally ill mother, I got the job.'

'I see,' Gray said smoothly.

'If you're thinking it was because he fancied me—'

'Knowing Jason, I must admit that the thought had crossed my mind.'

'I was given the post because of my experience.'

A gleam in his eye, he drawled, 'I don't doubt it.'

Colour tingeing her cheeks, she told him angrily, 'I'd been my father's personal assistant for well over a year.'

'Ah!'

'It was a job I enjoyed.'

'And, after Bowman Ferris changed hands, I take it you continued to enjoy working for Jason?'

'I did. But now I have to leave.'

'Why do you have to leave? So long as your work is still up to scratch there can be no possible grounds for getting rid of you. If by any chance he tried, you could always appeal directly to Philip Lorne.'

Tightly, she said, 'You don't understand—I *want* to leave. As things are, none of us, particularly Lisa, likes the idea of Jason and me having to see each other on a regular basis.'

'Presumably you've managed to cope since your engagement came to an end?'

'I handed in my notice then, but Jason begged me to stay on, for his sake.'

Gray frowned. 'I don't quite see?'

'He said that in spite of all his precautions the rest of the staff knew we'd been "friendly", and if I left suddenly there was bound to be gossip that might reach his uncle's ears.'

'Hmm... So what did you do?'

'I agreed to stay on for a while—'

Almost savagely, Gray said, 'Jason has always traded on his looks and his charm to get exactly what he wants.' Then with a sigh, 'Go on.'

'But only if I could work for someone else... As luck would have it, Mrs Richardson, the Assistant Managing Director's PA, was absent on maternity leave. Jason arranged for me to take her place temporarily, and his own secretary to do my work until Miss Swensen returned.

'It didn't stop a few tongues wagging, but when it became clear that we'd stayed on friendly terms the speculation died down.'

'And how do matters stand now?'

'I handed in my resignation last month, ready to leave as soon as Mrs Richardson and Miss Swensen came back. They're both due to return to work next Monday, so I won't need to go in again.'

Hearing the bleakness in her voice, Gray asked, 'Have you another post lined up?'

'Not yet. There don't seem to be many jobs going. But Jason has given me good references, so I'll find an opening somewhere.'

'How long have you been working?'

'I joined Bowman Ferris when I left college two years ago.'

'Why?'

When she looked at him blankly, he asked, 'Wouldn't your father have given you an allowance?'

'Oh, yes, he offered me one.'

'Why didn't you take it?'

'I didn't need an allowance. I wanted to work.'

His tone bland, Gray observed, 'The other two ladies seem to prefer a leisurely existence.'

'Surely that's up to them,' Rebecca said steadily. 'I'd always intended to have a career. That's why I chose to go to a business college.'

'If she hadn't got married, would your stepsister have gone to college?'

When the subject had once been mentioned, Lisa had looked disdainful. 'Why on earth should I want to join the ranks of scruffy, poverty-stricken students? I don't need a career. I've every intention of getting myself a rich husband.'

Displaying an uncanny accuracy, Gray queried, 'Or perhaps she was more interested in trawling the social waters in the hope of catching a good-looking, unattached, hopefully generous millionaire?'

Stiffly, Rebecca said, 'Since Lisa left school she's been helping Helen with her various committees and charity lunches.'

'Bully for her.' He sounded anything but impressed. Then thoughtfully, 'I notice you don't call your stepmother "Mother".'

'She's never wanted me to. When she and Dad got married, she was barely nineteen.'

'And you were how old?'

'Seven.'

'So your stepsister was just two?'

'Yes.'

'How did you get on with your stepmother?'

'Quite well.' That was something of an exaggeration. Though Helen had seldom been unkind to her, at the best she'd felt tolerated, provided she stayed in the background.

'I heard a whisper that she's always put her own daughter first.'

'It's understandable,' Rebecca said simply. 'I can't blame her for that.'

'What *can* you blame her for? Apart from today's bitchy remarks?'

'Nothing really…'

'The "really" convinces me there's *something*.'

'She's put Elmslee Manor on the market,' Rebecca said in a rush.

'I see. Did she give a reason?'

'She said it's too big for her. And of course, even apart from the mortgage repayments, it takes a lot of upkeep—' Rebecca stopped short, biting her lip, then burst out, 'But my father would have *hated* the idea. Elmslee has been in the family for generations, and he wouldn't have dreamt of parting with it. He loved the old place.'

'I take it you do too?'

'Yes.' She sighed. 'But there's nothing I can do. He willed it to Helen.'

'I see. So you have plenty of grounds for disliking her?'

'I *don't* dislike her. At the very least, she made Dad happy.'

'Your loyalty is admirable. If a trifle misplaced.'

Rebecca shook her head. 'I owe her a lot. After my mother ran away with another man, my father grew morose and started to drink heavily. I don't know what might have happened if he hadn't met Helen. They helped each other.

'She was in despair too. Her boyfriend had taken what little money they had and disappeared, abandoning her and the child, and leaving nothing but a pile of unpaid bills.

'A bare six weeks after she and Dad met they were married quietly, and he brought her to live at Elmslee. A year later he adopted Lisa.'

'Did you dislike having a new stepmother?'

'No. Though I'd loved my own mother very much she had never cared about me, and Dad seemed more settled than he'd been for years.'

'You weren't jealous of your stepsister?'

'No.'

Only once had she shown any sign of jealousy, and then Helen had sent her to her room in disgrace. It had been a salutary lesson, and she had never allowed herself to be jealous again.

'I've always been fond of Lisa.' Firmly, she added, 'I still am.'

'Even though she stole your fiancé?'

'You make it sound deliberate.'

'Wasn't it?'

As she hesitated, he said, 'So you think it was.' Adding curiously, 'Didn't you fight for him?'

'No.'

After she'd seen them together it had never occurred to her to even try. Her pride wouldn't have allowed her to.

'You just let her take him?'

When she stayed silent, he said thoughtfully, 'Though perhaps you were sensible. Someone as fickle as Jason isn't worth fighting for.'

'How can you be so disloyal?' she cried. 'You're supposed to be his friend.'

'It happens to be the truth,' Gray observed, his voice dispassionate.

'A fine friend you are!'

'I've always had his best interests at heart.'

As he reached to pour more wine it occurred to her vaguely that, though he was keeping her glass topped up, he was drinking little himself.

As though reading her thoughts, he explained, 'I'll be driving back to London later.'

So he wasn't a house guest. Which was odd, if he'd travelled all the way from the States...

'Speaking of hearts,' he pursued after a moment, 'when did Jason manage to lose his to your stepsister and break yours?'

'Last Easter.'

Any other time she wouldn't have answered such an ironically phrased question, but the amount of champagne she had drunk was succeeding in undermining her natural reticence.

'How did it happen?'

'Helen said they would like to meet Jason and see my ring.'

'Had you been engaged for long?'

Rebecca swallowed hard. 'Two months.'

'I didn't see your engagement announced in any of the papers.'

'It was never put in.'

'Why not? I would have thought your stepmother was the kind to fly to the social pages and spread the good news.'

'Unless she was cherishing fond hopes, even then, of her own daughter supplanting you.'

'It wasn't like that at all,' Rebecca denied. 'As a matter of fact it was Jason himself who wasn't keen to have it put in the papers. He preferred our engagement to be...unofficial.'

Slipping the ring onto her finger, he had said with charming insouciance, 'You can break the news to your own family if you want to, but I'll need time to talk Uncle Pip round, and I'd like the pair of you to meet before we tell the world.'

'Any particular reason for wanting it kept under wraps?' Gray asked.

'I think he was concerned that his ogre of an uncle might

not approve of him getting engaged to his PA. But if you and Jason are quite close I'm surprised you don't already know all this.'

'I'm afraid he isn't very good at keeping in touch,' Gray said smoothly. 'And, apart from the odd flying visit to London, I've been over in the States for a couple of years.'

Making the connection, she asked, 'You work for Finance International?'

'That's right.'

She wondered why he hadn't said so earlier, when he went on, 'Knowing what company gossip's like, I would have expected the news of your engagement to have filtered through. Especially if you wore your ring at the office.'

'I didn't. Jason asked me not to, so I wore it on a chain round my neck.'

'The whole thing sounds a bit hole-and-corner,' Gray observed sardonically, and watched as her cheeks turned pink.

'It was simply that he wanted time to talk his Uncle Pip round, and for the two of us to meet, before the engagement became public knowledge.'

But as far as she was aware, Jason had never even mentioned the engagement to Philip Lorne, much less arranged a meeting.

Seeing the look on Gray's face, she began defensively, 'I know the whole thing must sound ridiculous when Jason's twenty-three—'

'It does, rather.'

'But he was just six when his father was killed in an accident, and his mother died when he was barely fifteen. His uncle was made his guardian, and has been virtually running his life since then.

'Apparently Philip Lorne can be quite formidable, that's why Jason likes to keep on the right side of him and not rock the boat.'

Seeing the faint expression of contempt on Gray's face,

she said sharply, 'Don't think for a minute that it's cowardice—'

Pouring more champagne into her glass, he queried, 'So what would you call it? Expediency?'

Ignoring the blatant mockery, she hurried to defend her ex-fiancé. 'As well as Finance International, Philip Lorne controls all his late sister's business interests. Although Jason has a generous allowance, his uncle holds the purse strings, apparently for as long as he sees fit.'

'I'm well aware of the facts and the family history, of course,' Gray said, his voice dry. 'Though I hadn't appreciated that his uncle was quite such an ogre.'

'As Philip Lorne is based in New York, you know him presumably?'

'Yes, I know him.'

'What kind of man is he?' she asked curiously.

'He has a reputation for being a tough, but fair, businessman. I believe he's well-respected—'

'No, I mean what do you *personally* know about him?'

'I know he works very long hours, doesn't suffer fools gladly, cares about the environment and gives to charity.'

'What about his private life?'

'He likes to keep his private life just that.'

'I take it he's a very wealthy man?'

'You could say that. Though on the whole he lives fairly quietly, prefers to go about without being recognised, and hates publicity.'

'Would you say he was a violent man?'

'No, I wouldn't. What makes you ask?'

'It seems he once threatened to turn his young wife over his knee. What made it worse was that she was pregnant at the time.'

'Who told you that?'

'Jason. It happened quite a few years ago when he was just a teenager, but he still remembers it.'

Rebecca shivered. 'I thought Philip Lorne sounded an ab

solute brute. I was glad to know he wasn't coming to the wedding.'

'Was he invited?'

She shook her head. 'Jason said he wouldn't approve, and he'd prefer to face him when the whole thing was a *fait accompli*…'

Realising belatedly that her tongue was running away with her, she pulled herself up. 'I'm sorry. I really shouldn't be telling you all this.'

His voice without expression, Gray said, 'I'm finding it most interesting. Just for the record, do you happen to know *why* Lorne threatened his wife?'

'It was something to do with a family heirloom, a ring, she was wearing without his permission.'

'If that was all, I would most certainly agree with your assessment.'

Putting a hand on his arm, she gave him a pleading glance. 'For Jason's sake, I wouldn't like any of this to get back to Philip Lorne.'

'I promise I won't say a word.' Then casually, 'By the way, what happened to *your* ring when the engagement ended?'

'I gave it back to Jason, of course.'

'He didn't say you could keep it?'

'I wouldn't have kept it. Who wants a bitter reminder like that?'

Proving that he knew a great deal about Jason's affairs, Gray responded ironically, 'Apparently his previous fiancées did.'

CHAPTER TWO

'OR PERHAPS you didn't know he'd had any?'

Lifting her chin with an air of defiance, Rebecca said, 'Yes, I knew he'd been engaged twice before.'

She had heard it through the office grapevine the very same day she had accepted Jason's ring and his proposal of marriage.

'And it didn't worry you?' Gray asked.

'Not particularly.'

That wasn't strictly true. It had worried her enough to turn down Jason's plea that they should move in together.

Learning the reason for her refusal, he had first been angry, and then apologetic, saying, 'I suppose I should have told you myself. But as far as I was concerned it was of no great importance, and I was scared of losing you.'

She had been too much in love to want to doubt him.

'I must say I'm surprised,' Gray remarked, after a moment. 'If it was a stable, long-lasting relationship you were hoping for...?'

'Of course it was.'

'Surely a series of short-lived engagements couldn't be described as a good omen?'

'Hardly *a series*,' she said coldly. 'And Jason explained how they had both been...well...in the nature of experiments.'

Gray raised a sardonic brow. 'Really?'

'I believe his exact words were, ''Youthful ventures intended more to test the waters of matrimony than with any serious intention of swimming.'''

'And how did you interpret that?'

'I'm sorry?'

'I'm sure you don't lack intelligence, so it must be true that love makes people blind.'

'I don't know what you're getting at.'

'Didn't it sound as though he lacked commitment? As though he regarded those previous engagements as just another fling?'

'It did cross my mind,' she admitted.

Swallowing more champagne, she added unsteadily, 'But he assured me that I was quite different. He said he wanted to marry me so we could spend the rest of our lives together.'

But after a few short weeks, all that had changed.

To Rebecca's chagrin, her eyes filled with tears.

She tried desperately not to blink, but a single fat teardrop spilt over, rolled down her cheek and plopped into her hand as it lay, palm uppermost, in her lap.

Picking up her hand, Gray raised it to his lips and, delicately, with the tip of his tongue, collected the tear.

The intimacy of the gesture shook her, and she sat as though turned to stone, her amber eyes fixed on his lean, attractive face.

After a long moment, strangely breathless, she withdrew her hand, and looked anywhere but at him.

'Of course he'd have to *say* that,' Gray observed cynically. 'But in my opinion, when it came to marriage, Jason was in no hurry to let any woman pin him down.'

'He married Lisa,' Rebecca pointed out.

'Yes. It seems he more than met his match when it came to your stepsister...

'Incidentally, though you mentioned the change of heart came at Easter, you still haven't told me exactly how it happened.'

Once again he refilled her glass.

Reluctant to talk about it, but unhappily aware that she'd gone too far not to, Rebecca took another drink and began, 'Helen had arranged to have a small house party at Elmslee.

She asked me to come down and join them, and bring Jason.'

Neither of them had particularly wanted to go, but Helen had been so pressing that it had been almost impossible to say no.

'So you don't live here?' Gray asked curiously.

'I left home when I went to college.'

'And you didn't come back?'

'No.'

'Why not, if you all got on so well? Living in the country too quiet?'

'Not at all, I love the country, I always have. But as I was working in London, it made more sense to rent a small flat there.'

Her father had urged her to come back and live at Elmslee, suggesting eagerly that she could travel to and from the office with him. At first she had been sorely tempted, but Helen's cool reception of the idea had made her turn it down and plump for complete independence.

'So that's what you did?'

'Yes.'

'So when you and Jason were invited to Elmslee for Easter, you weren't living together?'

'No.'

'I can only presume you were holding out for a wedding ring first?'

Watching her expressive face, he smiled with quiet triumph. 'Whang in the gold, I see…'

Rebecca sighed. As soon as Jason's engagement ring was on her finger he had redoubled his efforts to get her to live with him.

Truth to tell, she had desperately wanted to. It was the recollection of his previous short-lived engagements that had made her cautious. Fearing that if she gave in too easily she might lose him, she had held back.

But she had still lost him.

If only she had agreed to at least sleep with him, things might have been different, she thought sadly.

Or, then again, they might not.

From first meeting Lisa, he had only too clearly been bowled over by her blonde beauty and her curvaceous figure.

'She's an absolute stunner,' he had said admiringly, 'a real pocket-Venus. You and she are total opposites.'

Then, realising too late how that must have sounded, he'd tacked on hastily, 'Though of course you're equally gorgeous, but in a different way.'

Rebecca had never, to the best of her knowledge, been described as pretty, let alone gorgeous.

Tall and slender, she'd been blessed with good bone-structure, almond eyes, even white teeth and a flawless skin. Even so, she knew herself to be no beauty. Her nose was too strong, her mouth too wide, her chin too firm.

Attractive, was most people's description. It was a description she was getting fed up with hearing...

Gray's voice broke into her thoughts, saying something she didn't catch.

Looking up fuzzily, she said, 'I beg your pardon?'

'I imagine Jason wasn't too pleased when you refused to move in with him. He likes his pleasure on tap, so to speak. He doesn't enjoy having to work for it, or having it doled out in small amounts.'

When she said nothing, he added thoughtfully, 'I take it your stepmother knew that you weren't actually living together?'

'Yes.'

'So she gave you separate rooms?'

'Yes.'

'Didn't you make any objection?'

'No.'

'I see...'

She was about to frame a protest, when he added, 'And

it might even have worked if you'd had the sense to keep him well away from your stepsister.'

Oddly enough, she hadn't seen that meeting as a threat. In retrospect, she knew how naïve and foolish she had been.

But they would have been bound to meet sooner or later, and she couldn't have coped with a marriage where she had to worry about every beautiful woman that crossed Jason's path.

As though reading her thoughts, Gray said satirically, 'Lock up your husband, and all that.'

'I wouldn't want...' She broke off.

'A husband you couldn't trust?' he hazarded.

'Yes.'

'Then, my dear Rebecca, you're better off out of it. As you know only too well, Jason isn't exactly renowned for his fidelity.'

Caught on the raw, she hit back. 'Jealous of his success with women?'

'What do you think?'

Though he was nowhere near as handsome as Jason, she felt oddly convinced that he would have no need to be jealous of him, or any man.

Unwilling to admit it, she said, 'Presumably you're here on your own today.'

'Don't you agree that's fortunate?' He smiled at her. A curiously intimate smile.

She put the little *frisson* that ran through her down to the fact that the air was appreciably cooler now the sun had set and dusk was creeping in.

'But I'm afraid we've strayed away from the point again,' he said, topping up her glass once more.

As she took a sip and looked at him a shade owlishly, he reminded her, 'You were about to tell me what happened at Easter.'

While he listened attentively, making an effort to dispel the tiredness that was creeping over her, she found herself telling this virtual stranger things she wouldn't have told her best friend.

'It was obvious from the start that Jason thought Lisa was stunning. In fact, he said as much. She seemed to like him, and several times—both the mornings we went riding, one evening at cards, and again when we played Murder—I found myself paired off with her current boyfriend, while they joined forces.'

Helen too had made quite a fuss of him, and clearly enjoying himself, Jason had remarked how pleased he was that they had decided to come.

Stupidly, Rebecca saw now, she had been glad that things were going so well.

'Go on,' Gray said.

'We had been planning to go back to London on Easter Monday, but because the rest of the party were staying until the following day Helen asked us to stay too, and Jason agreed.

'After dinner that evening we were in the middle of playing Charades when the strap on my watch broke. Jason said he would try to fix it for me later, and slipped it into his pocket.

'By the time we went upstairs to bed, we'd both forgotten about it. Jason kissed me goodnight at my bedroom door as usual, then went to his own room across the landing.

'It wasn't until I was about to take off my watch to shower that I remembered Jason still had it.

'The room Helen had given me had no clock, and because I always wear a watch I felt lost without one. After I'd showered and got ready for bed I pulled on a dressing gown and went to Jason's room to fetch it.'

She emptied her glass, and he took it from her and set it down on the bench.

'Go on,' he said again.

She took a deep breath. 'I tapped at his door. There was no answer, so I tapped again, but quietly, in case I disturbed anyone else. When there was still no answer, thinking he must be in the shower, I walked in…'

The words tailed off and she looked down at her lap, where her hands were clenched into fists.

'I take it your stepsister was there with him.'

'Yes,' she whispered.

They had been together on the bed, in a flurry of naked limbs and hoarse breathing. As she'd stood rooted to the spot, both of them had glanced up, their faces blind with passion.

She could still clearly recall how their expressions had altered. Jason's flushed, handsome face had looked startled and guilty, while Lisa's expression had changed to one of quiet triumph.

Without a word, Rebecca had turned and blundered away, stumbling in her haste to escape from the ugly little scene.

But she had carried it in her mind's eye like a video recording. One that she was unable to switch off; one that had replayed itself continuously until she thought she would go mad.

Peering at his companion in the gathering gloom, Gray asked, 'What did you do?'

'I went back to my room, but I couldn't sleep. Railton, the nearest town, has a twenty-four-hour taxi service, so at two o'clock in the morning, I packed my things and called a taxi.

'The following day I made myself go into the office to hand in my notice and give Jason his ring back. The rest you know.'

Gray frowned. 'I'm curious about one thing. How did you and your stepsister manage to stay friends?'

'Lisa was living in town—'

'With Jason presumably.'

'Yes. One day she called at my flat. She said she was sorry, she had only knocked at Jason's door to say goodnight, and somehow it had just happened.'

'But you didn't believe her?'

She shook her head.

'Tell me, what made you agree to be a bridesmaid?'

The sun had long since set, and with dusk pressing against the windows she was starting to feel distinctly cool in the short-sleeved silk dress.

Repressing a shiver, she answered, 'I didn't at first. In fact I'd booked a holiday in the Caribbean so I could avoid the wedding.'

'Why didn't you go on it?'

'When Helen found out, she was furious. She said that if I wasn't chief bridesmaid everyone would think there'd been a family split.'

'Would it have mattered what people thought?'

'That's what I asked.'

'And what did she say?'

Rebecca rubbed her hands up and down her bare arms while she made an effort to sort out the jumble of thoughts in her head.

'She said something like, "Jason's a well-to-do, titled man from a wealthy background. After Lisa and he are married we'll no doubt be moving in top society, and it might spoil everything if there was unkind talk."'

'I see,' Gray murmured, his voice sardonic. 'Well if your stepmother has those kind of expectations, perhaps her daughter should have set her cap at the organ-grinder.'

'The organ-grinder?' Rebecca echoed blankly.

'I'll explain it some time.' Seeing that she was beginning to shiver, he rose, adding decidedly, 'Time we were moving. It's starting to get cooler in here.'

She got to her feet and, as her head began to whirl, sat down again with a bump. 'You'd better go. The reception will be over now. They'll be wondering where you've got to.'

He laughed mirthlessly. 'I very much doubt it. Come on,

now, let's have you up and moving before you catch a chill in that dress.'

'I'll come in a minute or so. You go on.'

'No chance. I'll see you back to the house. You must be getting hungry.'

She shook her head.

'After so much champagne you probably need to eat, and before too long.'

'I don't want to eat. At least not *here*.' She was aware that she sounded panicky.

'Then what *do* you want?'

'I want to go back to London.'

'How did you get to Elmslee?'

Focusing with an effort, she told him, 'I came down with some family friends, but they'll be staying until tomorrow.'

'Shouldn't you do the same?'

'No,' she cried vehemently. 'I couldn't bear to. Not after what Helen said.'

Desperate now to be left on her own so she could gather herself, she added, 'You really ought to go. I'll be all right... Honestly, I will.'

Unconvinced, he said, 'Let me see you stand up.'

'I'm not sure I can just at the moment,' she admitted. 'When I stand, I go dizzy.'

'When did you last eat?'

'I can't remember.'

'Lunch?'

Shivering in earnest now, she said, 'I didn't have any lunch.'

'Breakfast?'

'Only coffee.'

'Hell!' he exclaimed softly. 'I'm not surprised it's gone to your head. And it's no wonder you're feeling cold.'

'I just wish you'd go and leave me.'

'You're in no fit state to be left.'

Enunciating every word with care, she said, 'When I've

sat for a little while longer I'll be quite capable of walking back to the house.'

'Then what will you do?'

'As soon as I've got back to my room and changed, I'll ring for a taxi.'

'Do you seriously think you'll be able to cope on your own?'

She *had* to. Haughtily, she said, 'Of course I will.' The effect was spoiled by the fact that, in spite of all her efforts, she was having a job to stay upright.

Smoothly, he said, 'I think it would be better if I saw you safely back home.' Putting an arm around her, he urged her to her feet.

Angry with herself, knowing she should have had more sense than to drink so much champagne, she tried to pull free. 'Thank you, but I don't need any help.'

'Don't be foolish, of course you need help,' he said curtly.

'I can manage,' she insisted, and clenched her teeth to stop them chattering.

'Very well.' He removed his arm.

She made a valiant attempt to stand unaided, but was forced to clutch at him.

'Still convinced you can manage?' he asked.

Her legs buckling under her ignominiously, she sank back onto the bench.

With an air of I-told-you-so, he took off his jacket, put it around her shoulders, slipped her arms into the sleeves and fastened the buttons to keep it in place.

It half buried her and the sleeves hung over her hands, but it still held his body heat, and she found the warmth curiously comforting. Leaning her head back against the wooden wall, she closed her eyes.

'Don't go to sleep.' He tapped her cheek with a none-too-gentle finger. 'We need to be moving.'

When the heavy lids lifted, he helped her to her feet once more.

'Please, I—'

'No more arguments.' Putting an arm around her, he began to steer her towards the door. 'It's high time I got you back to the house.'

'I'm not your res...res...' She made another attempt. 'Your responsibility.'

Flatly, he said, 'It's my fault you're tipsy.'

But, while she was undeniably tipsy, one small part of her mind remained stone-cold sober, and, standing aloof, watched and judged with critical detachment.

She had been stupid to let her stepmother's comments throw her. If only she had ignored them, stayed cool and aloof, kept her dignity...

But she hadn't. And now it was too late. If anyone saw her obviously the worse for drink, she would look like a complete loser. Spineless and pathetic.

She felt ashamed, totally humiliated in a way that even Helen's spiteful remarks had been unable to make her feel.

As, one arm supporting her, Gray reached for the latch, she begged, 'Please stop...'

'Feeling sick?' he enquired.

'No.'

'Thank the lord for that.'

'But I don't—'

'If necessary I'll carry you.'

He opened the door and, holding it with his foot, said firmly, 'Let's go.'

'Oh, please, can't we wait? I don't want to risk meeting anyone.'

'There's no point in waiting any longer. If we go now, there's a chance that most of the guests will still be congregating in the marquee.'

Even in her panic-stricken state it made sense, and she let herself be chivvied outside and helped down the steps.

The air was cool and fresh, the clear, dark-blue sky pricked with stars. A faint breeze carried the scent of honeysuckle.

Thankfully that part of the garden appeared to be deserted, and only the faint sound of music drifted their way.

'All ready?' he asked.

'Yes.'

But when she tried to walk her sense of balance had totally deserted her, and even with Gray taking most of her weight her rubbery legs refused to work.

'I can't see us getting far at this rate,' he remarked calmly, 'so you'd better put your arms round my neck.'

Lurching a little, she obeyed, linking her hands inside the sleeves of his jacket.

A moment later he was lifting her effortlessly. His strength was as comforting as his warmth, and, her head against his shoulder, she gave up the struggle and let him take control.

She couldn't remember ever being carried before, and the feel of the powerful male body she was being held against, and the solid bone and muscle beneath her cheek, stirred her senses in a way she had simply never envisaged.

Dimly she realised that it must be the champagne that was lowering her inhibitions and making her feel this way.

His step brisk and his breathing even, carrying her as easily as if she were a child, he said, 'I propose that we head for the rear of the house. If we go in the back way there should be less chance of us being seen.'

Avoiding the floodlit areas, Gray skirted the old walled garden, and as they got nearer to the main lawn he began to move with even greater care.

Though the sound of the orchestra playing and a buzz of conversation was still coming from the brightly lit marquee, thanks to the space-heaters and the beauty of the evening, some guests had elected to sit outside.

As they got closer the pungent scent of cigar smoke, mingled with coffee, wafted towards them.

They were just drawing level with the entrance to the marquee, when two couples came out and, laughing and talking, headed in their direction.

Gray muttered something beneath his breath, and in one fluid movement set her down, her back against the nearest tree trunk, and, shielding her from the possibility of prying eyes, bent to kiss her.

Rebecca hadn't been kissed since the night her engagement had ended so disastrously, and, though it was a chaste kiss, meant merely for show, the feel of his mouth on hers had the strangest effect.

She was vaguely aware that the little group were quite close, but, as her lips parted beneath the slight pressure of his, somehow it no longer seemed to matter.

As she clung to him, dizzy and helpless, he continued to kiss her while the foursome passed by, still talking. Only when their voices had faded into the distance did he raise his head.

Glancing around, he said softly, 'The coast seems to be clear momentarily, so we'd better make tracks. If we keep to the far side of this yew hedge, we should be out of sight for most of the way.'

Lifted high in his arms once more, she was carried through an archway of yew to another expanse of lawn.

His footsteps made no sound on the grass, and with the faint scent of his aftershave in her nostrils, and the feel of his silk shirt beneath her cheek, she found herself experiencing a kind of drifting unreality, as if the whole thing was just a dream.

'I take it there's a way through near the house?'

His question made her open her eyes, and rousing herself, she answered, 'Yes, there's another archway just before you get to the orangery.'

'That's useful. I've parked by the orangery.'

As they approached the house, even through the sheltering yew, they could see it was ablaze with lights. 'Where exactly is your room?' he queried. 'Is it easy to get to?'

Struggling against an overwhelming desire to let go and sink into sleep, she made herself concentrate. 'It's the first door on the right at the top of the main staircase.'

'Sounds comparatively simple.'

As they reached the archway, he added wryly, 'The only thing is, we appear to have left it a bit late for getting in and out unseen.'

To Rebecca's consternation she saw that the place was alive with people coming and going in ones and twos and small groups.

'Which leaves our present situation open to all kinds of misinterpretation,' he added grimly.

'Whatever are we going to do?' she moaned.

'Would you prefer to simply get in the car and go?'

'Yes... No...'

'Which?'

'I can't. The key to my flat is in my handbag.'

'Then perhaps you'd better wait in the car while I go and fetch it.'

'Oh, thank you,' she said fervently.

'Luckily, what with arriving late, I'm parked a fair way from the house.'

Moving with caution, he kept beyond the range of the lights until they reached the end of the line of parked cars.

'Here we are.' Setting her down carefully beside a silver Jaguar, he unlocked it and helped her into the front passenger seat.

'Just in case anyone walks past, it might be as well to take off your headdress. Being light-coloured, it tends to be noticeable.'

For a moment or two she fumbled ineffectually, hampered by nerveless fingers and the over-long jacket sleeves.

'Let me.' Stooping, he felt for the pins that held it in place and began to remove them one by one.

'There.' He lifted the circlet of fresh flowers free, letting the long, silky hair tumble around her shoulders. 'Presumably you don't want to keep it?'

'No,' she said emphatically.

'If we were in Hawaii you could give it to Pele. As we're not...' He sent the circlet skimming like a Frisbee into the night.

Though the whole thing seemed completely surreal, somehow the gesture lifted her spirits and made her giggle like a schoolgirl.

Dropping the pins into the door pocket, he queried, 'I imagine you have an overnight case or something I can put your things into?'

The alcohol was taking even more of a hold, making her thoughts as sluggish as wasps in treacle, and it was a moment or two before she was able to say, 'Yes... But if you can bring my bag I don't mind if you leave everything else. I mean, if someone sees you, won't it look a bit odd if you come down carrying a case?'

'Not half as odd as it'll look if I come down carrying a lady's handbag. But if I put everything into a case, I could simply be a guest who's decided not to stay after all.'

Her voice slurred, she asked, 'What will you do if there are still a lot of people about?'

'Walk in as if I owned the place,' he answered cheerfully. 'There must be plenty of house guests who won't necessarily know one another, so I'm unlikely to be challenged unless I'm unlucky enough to run into your stepmother.

'Now, are you warm enough? Or shall I leave the engine running?'

'I'm warm enough, thank you.'

He slammed the car door quietly, and she watched him walk away, only his white shirt visible until he got within range of the lights.

This wedding couldn't have been much fun for *him*, she thought. Not only had he missed the reception, but he was also going to drive back to London without even speaking to his friend.

He was a strange, complex man, sardonic and abrasive, bordering on cruel at times, yet he'd gone out of his way to help and care for her...

Resting her head against the leather upholstery, she closed her eyes with a sigh.

A movement beside her, and the muted roar of the engine springing into life, made her lift her head and open bleary eyes.

Reaching across to fasten her seat belt, Gray answered her unspoken question. 'Everything's fine. All your belongings are in the boot.'

'Thank you...' Almost before the words were out, she was fast asleep again.

'Wake up, sleeping beauty.'

Eyes still closed, she tried to brush away the intrusive fingers that were stroking her cheek.

'We're home.' He'd found her address amongst her things and driven straight there.

She didn't care. All she wanted was to be left in peace. She tried to say so, but the voice was insisting, 'Come on, wake up,' and the fingers were no longer stroking, but slapping lightly.

Feeling aggrieved, she opened heavy lids and realised dazedly that they were parked in front of Prince Albert's Court, and that Gray was standing by her side with the car door open.

'That's better,' he murmured. 'Now, let's see how you are on your feet.'

He hauled her out, and, finding she was like a rag doll,

half carried her across the pavement and through the main entrance into a bare hallway with doors on either side.

It was an unprepossessing block in a drab neighbourhood, and, presumably in a half-hearted attempt to brighten the place, all the doors had been painted different colours.

As her head began to droop, he said sharply, 'Don't go to sleep again until I know which is your flat.'

'That one.' She pointed an unsteady finger at a mustard-coloured door on their right.

'Nice and close, which is just as well.'

'The key…' she began.

'It's all right, I've already found it.' Supporting her with one arm, he unlocked the door.

Having helped her inside, he lowered her onto the couch and, leaving the door a little ajar, went out again to bring in her belongings.

When he returned her eyes flickered open momentarily, then closed once more.

Coming to give her a little shake, he reminded her, 'You really ought to have something to eat.'

'Couldn't eat…'

'What about some coffee?'

She shook her head.

'In that case the best place for you is bed, and the sooner you're tucked in the better.'

He helped her into the bedroom and sat her down on the edge of the double bed.

Catching a blurred glimpse of herself in the mirror, she felt a sudden revulsion at the sight of the gleaming necklace of cultured pearls that had been the bridegroom's gift to the bridesmaids.

Pearls for tears.

Having tried, and failed, to unfasten it, desperate to be rid of the thing, she began to tug at it.

'Whoa there,' Gray cautioned. 'Let me.'

He unfastened the necklace and tossed it onto the dressing

table, then, crouching to slip off her shoes, asked, 'What about your clothes?'

Gathering her dignity, she said, 'I can manage.'

Watching her struggle ineffectually with the small covered buttons that fastened the bodice of her dress, he suggested, 'It might be a whole lot easier to sleep in it.'

'No.'

'Then you'd best let me help you.'

He unfastened the buttons, and, easing the dress from beneath her, lifted it over her head. 'There, you can always sleep in the rest.'

'No. I couldn't bear to.' She wanted to be rid of all her wedding things right now, this minute.

While she swam in and out of consciousness, he helped her off with the remainder of her clothes and settled her head on the pillow.

Pulling up the duvet, he remarked, 'It's been a long day.'

A long day... Lisa's and Jason's wedding day... The worst day of her life...

And the worst night. Their wedding night and the start of their honeymoon.

Would they be going to Paris? Jason had promised to take *her* to Paris. They had been going to do so much. But now she was all alone, with nothing and no one in her life.

Unsure whether or not she'd spoken the words aloud or merely thought them, she found slow tears rolling down her face.

'And it's obviously been too much for you.' Sitting on the edge of the bed, he brushed a strand of hair away from her wet cheek.

His tenderness was her undoing, and she began to cry even harder.

'Don't cry, little one.'

'Why not?' she asked bitterly.

'Because if you cry I'll have to comfort you, and one thing can lead to another.'

Big eyes on his face, she sniffed dolefully.

'Don't cry any more now. By tomorrow things may not seem quite so bad.'

He sounded kind and caring, and, knowing that Jason didn't care a fig about her, she was pathetically grateful that someone did.

As his dark face swam in and out of focus, she caught hold of his hand. 'Thank you.'

'Goodnight and sweet dreams.' He rose to his feet.

Still clinging to his hand, she begged hoarsely, 'Don't leave me. Please don't leave me. I don't want to be on my own tonight...'

CHAPTER THREE

WHEN Rebecca first stirred and began to slowly surface, her mind was a complete and utter blank. She hadn't the faintest idea how she had got to bed, or what had happened the previous day.

After a while, insubstantial images began to swirl and eddy in her consciousness, appearing and disappearing like wraiths in a mist.

Lisa and Jason standing in church together and being declared man and wife.

Helen, wearing a peacock-blue hat trimmed with iridescent feathers, saying, so everyone could hear, 'Of course poor Rebecca's terribly disappointed...'

Herself fleeing to her childhood sanctuary to lick her wounds in private.

Then a tall dark-haired stranger appearing with a bottle of champagne and saying drily, 'I've been told that women always cry at weddings, but don't you think this is overdoing it a bit?'

Squeezing her eyes tightly closed, as if that would stop the images appearing, she groaned as she remembered how, the champagne loosening her tongue, she had told him things she wouldn't normally have told a living soul.

Oh, how could she have been stupid enough to get tipsy? She had made a complete fool of herself, and if it hadn't been for...Gray Gallagher...yes, that was his name, *everyone* would have known it.

Though it was like looking through a glass darkly, she half remembered him carrying her back up the garden...kissing her...helping her into his car...then taking off

43

her headdress and sending it skimming into the night, before going back to the house to fetch her things.

She could recall nothing after that.

But he must have seen her safely home, as she was in her own bed and her overnight case and bag were on the chest.

There was a lot to thank him for.

If she ever saw him again.

Knowing what he must think of her, she found herself hoping fervently that she *wouldn't* see him again. Such a meeting was bound to be desperately uncomfortable, to say the least.

But there should be no problem, she realised belatedly. He lived and worked in the States, so presumably, having flown in especially for the wedding, he'd go back now it was over.

Her thoughts growing muzzy, she closed her eyes again and lay drifting on the edge of sleep, until the sound of breakfast television from the next-door flat roused her.

What time was it? she wondered.

Peering blearily at her watch, she found it was gone eight o'clock.

Normally she was up and about well before seven. But, as though the past weeks of eating little and sleeping less had finally caught up with her, she felt mentally and physically exhausted, all her normal drive and energy missing.

Even so, she should make a move.

But what was there to get up for? It wasn't as though she had a job to go to.

In that case she should be out looking for one, her conscience responded promptly. It wouldn't be too long before she ran out of money.

The grim reality of the thought shocked her into action, and, her ash-brown hair tumbling round her shoulders, she struggled to sit up.

It wasn't until her head stopped spinning that she realised

she was naked. She had no recollection of taking off her clothes, but her bridesmaid's dress and undies were folded over a chair.

If she had been *compos mentis* enough to fold her things so neatly, why hadn't she put on a nightie? She always wore a nightie...

Her head throbbing dully and her mouth desert-dry, she gave up the puzzle and, throwing back the duvet, swung her feet to the floor.

She was heading for the bathroom, when she noticed something that stopped her in her tracks.

A creature of habit, she invariably slept with a single pillow, and on the right-hand side of the bed. Now the left-hand side was rumpled, and there was an extra pillow.

As she stared at it stupidly, she realised two things. It was the spare pillow that normally lived in the top of the wardrobe, and it bore the imprint of a head.

Feeling as though she had been kicked in the solar plexus, she sank down on the nearest chair. It *couldn't* be what it looked like, she thought, even as she understood that it *could*, and undoubtedly *was*.

She began to shake like a leaf.

No, surely he wouldn't have done such a thing?

Or would he?

What did she know of the man? Very little except that he lived in the States, worked for Philip Lorne, and was a friend of Jason's.

Of his morals she knew less than nothing.

But the mere fact that he'd taken advantage of her drunken state and then cleared out spoke volumes.

As the full horror of the situation sank in, she whispered, 'Oh, dear God.'

It was savage retribution for being stupid enough to get drunk, and trust a perfect stranger.

Several minutes passed before she was able to get up and,

stomach churning, knees like jelly, make her way to the bathroom.

Drops of water were still clinging to the patterned glass of the shower-stall, while the fresh scent of some masculine shower gel hung on the air. A damp towel had been draped over the laundry basket, and a disposable toothbrush discarded in the bin.

He'd obviously made himself thoroughly at home before leaving, she thought bleakly.

Disliking the idea of standing where he had stood, but desperate to feel clean again, she forced herself to ignore the sense of shock and outrage, and step into the shower.

Watching water and bubbles of peach-blossom shampoo cascade down her slender body, she noted—in an oddly detached way, as though this creamy flesh wasn't really hers—that it bore not the slightest sign of marks or bruises.

But presumably she had been either too far gone to struggle, or already unconscious when he stripped off her clothes.

Despite the steamy heat she went cold, every nerve in her body screaming a protest. It took a moment or two to gather herself enough to carry on.

When she had dried her hair she pulled on a towelling robe and, sinking onto a stool to clean her teeth, caught sight of herself in the mirror.

Staring abstractedly at the white-faced woman who stared mutely back at her, she wondered, what was she to do?

But there was nothing she could do.

So, rather than sit here brooding, she decided, she would go out and make a fresh effort to find another job. At least that would be a positive step. It should help to take her mind off what had happened.

Feeling a fraction more cheerful, she brushed her hair and coiled it into a neat chignon, before making up with care.

Then, her legs still feeling shaky, she forced herself to go back to the bedroom.

Averting her eyes from the bed, she found a silky top in

mint-green and a stone-coloured trouser suit, and, suddenly
desperate to get out of the flat, dressed with all speed.

Common sense told her that she ought to have some
breakfast before she went, but the thought of food made her
stomach churn even more.

Though she *was* in need of a drink.

Going through to the kitchen, she put on the kettle and
with unsteady hands made a pot of coffee and poured herself
a mug of the fragrant brew.

She had just added milk and a spoonful of sugar and sat
down at the table to drink it, when she heard the sound of
the front door opening and closing.

A moment later the tall, broad-shouldered figure of Gray
Gallagher filled the kitchen doorway.

The formal garb of yesterday, with its matching shirt and
tie was gone. Wearing smart casuals and a short car coat
unbuttoned and swinging loose, he looked completely at his
ease.

'Mmm...' He sniffed appreciatively. 'Thought I could
smell coffee.'

While she sat speechless, he strolled over and helped himself to a mugful, as though he lived here and had every
right.

'I wondered if you'd be up. You were still asleep when
I left.'

As he spoke he studied her, surprised afresh by her
beauty. A beauty he had only fully appreciated that morning
when he had stood looking down at her sleeping face.

Yesterday he had seen her as attractive, with a lovely,
passionate mouth and fascinating amber eyes. Now he noticed the shape of her face, her delicate ears, her pure bone
structure.

Dropping into a chair opposite, he began to drink his
coffee, his eyes still appraising her.

Her heart racing suffocatingly fast, Rebecca found her
voice and demanded, 'How did you get in?'

'I borrowed your key in case you were still asleep when I got back.'

'I didn't expect you back.'

He lifted a dark brow. 'Why not?'

'After what happened...' Her words tailed off.

With a wry smile, he observed, 'I'm rather surprised you remember what happened.'

'I don't,' she admitted. 'But it's quite obvious.'

Picking up her agitation, he asked mildly, 'What's quite obvious?'

'You must have undressed me!'

When he failed to deny it, she burst out angrily, 'You took advantage of me.'

His good-looking face the picture of innocence, he enquired, 'In what way?'

'You know perfectly well!'

'If you mean we slept together...'

'Are you trying to pretend we didn't?'

'No.'

'You're a swine.' Her voice shook.

Smoothly, he enquired, 'What makes you think I'm solely to blame?'

Pushing away the awful thought that she might have invited it, she said raggedly, 'If you'd had a shred of decency, you'd have gone. Left me alone.'

'I was about to, but you pleaded with me to stay.'

'No! I don't believe it.'

'Your exact words were, "Please don't leave me. I don't want to be on my own tonight."' For good measure, he added, 'You took hold of my hand and clung to me.'

Somewhere deep down it struck a chord, and, though she wanted to dismiss it all as lies, she couldn't doubt that he was telling the truth.

Unable to repudiate it, she retorted, 'You must have realised that I was still too drunk to know what I was doing or saying.'

'Drunk or sober, it was clear that you were in need of some…company.'

'If you knew what kind of woman I am,' she cried bitterly, 'you'd know perfectly well that I don't go in for that kind of *company*, or one-night stands.'

'As I don't know what kind of woman you are, I'm afraid I wasn't able to judge.'

'So you went ahead and slept with me!'

'Are you using the words ''slept with'' as a euphemism for ''had sex with''?'

'Yes, I am.'

'Then the answer's no, I didn't.'

'You didn't?' she echoed blankly.

'If you knew what kind of man I are, you'd know perfectly well that I don't go in for one-night stands either.'

Coldly, he went on, 'Nor do I enjoy ''sleeping with'' unconscious women. And believe me, a second or two after asking me to stay you were out for the count.'

With the beginnings of relief, but still needing some additional reassurance, she said, 'So you *didn't* sleep with me?'

'I could just say *no* again, but in the interests of accuracy it's a fact that I slept beside you in the same bed. That's all. Nothing more, nothing less.'

Remembering her naked state, she said, 'If that really is all, I don't understand why you went to the trouble of undressing me.'

Straight-faced, he said, 'It was no trouble.'

Watching her blush, he continued, 'But before you start accusing me of getting my kicks that way, it had been a long day for me too, and I was more than ready for some sleep versus hanky-panky.'

Flustered, she pointed out, 'I could have slept in my clothes.'

'After I'd unfastened your pearls I suggested that, but you

were desperate to get rid of all your wedding finery, so I helped you.'

Once again some faint recollection told her he spoke the truth.

'Apart from that, I never laid so much as a finger on you. Happy now?'

Crossly, she accused, 'At first you deliberately led me to believe the worst.'

When he merely looked at her, she demanded, 'Why?'

'It seemed to be what you *wanted* to believe.'

'I didn't want to believe anything of the kind,' she cried indignantly. 'I was absolutely *horrified*.'

Pulling a face, he complained, 'You said that in such a heartfelt way, I could quite easily end up with a complex. Or at the very least a severely dented ego…'

Against all expectations, she found herself laughing. Not only did it ease the tension, but it made her realise that she had barely smiled, let alone laughed, in many weeks.

'More coffee?' he queried, rising to his feet.

She nodded.

'Milk and sugar?'

'Milk and one sugar, please.'

It was the first time she had been calm enough to look at him objectively, and while he poured their coffee she studied him, covertly weighing him up.

He was even more attractive than she had realised, with a lean, strong-boned face and handsome eyes beneath dark, level brows.

His teeth were white and even, and his long, flexible mouth, with its austere upper lip and sensuous lower, aesthetically pleasing.

But apart from Gray Gallagher's looks and his physique there was something about him, something charismatic—a maturity, a quiet confidence—that gave him an air of authority and power. An air that, she felt sure, would turn most women on.

He glanced up suddenly, and, annoyed that she had been caught staring at him, she looked hastily away, a tinge of betraying pink rising in her cheeks.

When he just waited, leaving the ball in her court, she went back to one point that was still niggling. 'I don't understand why you stayed here last night.'

He passed her the replenished mug and sat down again, crossing his legs the way men did, one ankle resting casually on the opposite knee. 'You mean, if it wasn't simply to have my wicked way with you?'

Her colour deepening, she said crisply, 'As you weren't an overnight guest at Elmslee Manor, I presume you had a hotel booked.'

'I didn't, as a matter of fact.'

'Oh.'

'No, I wasn't in need of a free night's lodging.'

'I wasn't thinking any such thing...' she began, then stopped, realising by the gleam in his eye that he was angling for a rise.

'I have my own place.'

Startled, she said, 'Well, if you have your own place I really can't imagine why you stayed here. It's hardly the height of luxury.'

'You seemed to want me to stay and, as I felt guilty about the state you were in, I thought it best to keep an eye on you.'

Seeing how pale she still was beneath the make-up, he queried, 'How are you feeling this morning?'

'A bit rough, but probably better than I deserve.'

Noting, with an odd little flutter, that his handsome, heavily lashed eyes, which she had expected to be grey or light blue, were green flecked with gold, she took a deep breath and went on, 'I owe you an abject apology.'

He half shook his head, but she ploughed on determinedly, 'Firstly, for misjudging you, and secondly, for yesterday. You must have come over from the States especially for the wedding, and because of me you even missed the reception.'

'That was my choice,' he pointed out.

'But it means your journey has been a complete waste of time.'

A twinkle in his eye, he drawled, 'Oh, I wouldn't say that.'

She swallowed. 'Unless, of course, you have business in London?'

'Not at this precise moment.' An edge to his voice, he added, 'Though I will have in a couple of weeks.'

'So when do you go back to the States?'

'This morning.'

'Oh.' In spite of having earlier wished him gone, she felt a strange sense of disappointment. Doing her best to hide it, she said, 'Well, I hope you have a good flight back to New York.'

'I'm not going back to New York. At least, not at the moment.'

'I thought you lived there.'

'Yes, I do. But first I have a one-night stop-over in Boston for an urgent business meeting, then a trip to California.'

'Business or pleasure?'

'A bit of each. Finance International have just acquired a rundown vineyard in the Napa Valley, so I'm going over there to take a look at it and try to work out the potential.

'Mainly, however, I'm looking forward to a break. I haven't had a holiday since I've been in the States, so I'm hoping to take it easy and enjoy the sun for a couple of weeks before flying back to London.'

Then with no change of tone, so that at first she scarcely took in what he was saying, 'Why not come with me?'

'Come with you?' she echoed after a moment. 'You mean to California?'

'Why not?'

'I—I just couldn't,' she stammered.

'Have you ever been to California?'

'No.' The furthest she'd ever managed to get was to the Italian Alps on a cheap skiing break with some college friends.

'But you like travelling. You told me you'd booked a Caribbean holiday.'

'Yes, but I—'

'They both start with the letter C,' he pointed out quizzically, 'and if you go you might find you like California better.'

It had been one of her childhood dreams to someday see the west coast of America...

Snapping off the thought, she told herself not to be a fool. The mere idea of going to California with Gray Gallagher, a man she had thought of as rude and abrasive, was ridiculous.

But his attitude had changed, she realised. He no longer seemed so scathing, so deliberately cruel. In fact he'd been positively kind.

Even so...

She shook her head. 'I couldn't possibly go.'

'What is there to keep you in London? You've given up your job, so there's nothing to fill your days. Unless you *want* to sit and think of Lisa and Jason enjoying their honeymoon?'

Seeing the look on her face, he regretted his cruelty. It was like slapping a child.

His tone kinder, he observed, 'Now the marriage is a *fait accompli*, it's time you cut free, left the past behind you. Though this trip is no big deal, a complete change of scenery might be just what you need to take your mind off things.'

He sounded so down-to-earth that, from being unthinkable, it began to seem feasible.

When, trying to cope with the rush of excitement that threatened to overrule common sense, she said nothing, he urged, 'Go on, give me one good reason why you shouldn't come.'

Pulling herself together, she asked, 'You mean apart from the obvious one?'

He grinned appreciatively. 'The obvious one being that you're a "nice girl", and nice girls don't go away on holiday with strange men?'

'Exactly.'

'A somewhat dated outlook, yet in my book a commendable one. But apart from that?'

As she had absolutely no intention of going, it was absurd to have to give a reason. All the same she found herself doing it.

'For one thing I couldn't afford the air fare.'

'You wouldn't need to—I'm using the company jet.'

'And for another I must stay in London and keep looking for a job.' Unguardedly, she added, 'If I don't get one before too long I'll be in a mess.'

'You mean financially?'

Reluctantly, she answered, 'Yes.'

'Well, I have plenty of contacts both here and in the States, so don't worry about getting a job. I'll see you're fixed up as soon as we get back.

'And as far as this holiday is concerned you won't need to pay a penny.'

Seeing her expression, he said wryly, 'There are no strings attached, I assure you. I'm not asking you to share my bed.' A gleam of laughter in his green eyes, he added, 'Unless, of course, you want to—'

'I *don't* want to.'

'There you go,' he complained, 'denting my ego again. But seriously, there's a house that goes with the vineyard, so you can have your own room and simply come as my guest. At the end of the fortnight I'll bring you back to London.'

Letting go of one obstacle, she cited another. 'It might be
nore than your job's worth.'

'No one questions what I do. I have a completely free
and.'

And he must be fairly high up the ladder to have been
iven the use of the company jet. Still, she protested, 'But
f Philip Lorne found out...'

'So long as I'm getting the work done, he wouldn't con-
ern himself. And I think at the very least Finance
nternational owe you a holiday.

'Because of Jason you've lost out quite badly, and I know
.orne well enough to be sure that if he heard what had
appened he wouldn't be at all pleased with his nephew.'

'You won't tell him?' she asked quickly.

'It all depends.'

'On what?'

'On whether or not you decide to take up my offer.'

'That's blackmail.'

'Call it friendly persuasion.'

'If there are no strings attached, why do you want me to
ome?'

'Apart from the reasons I've already stated, when I'm not
vorking I like to have a companion, someone to share things
vith.'

Frowning, she wondered why a man with his kind of
)oks and charisma would need to use blackmail to get him-
elf a companion.

'If you wanted companionship, why didn't you bring a
irlfriend?' she asked.

'I don't happen to have one at the moment. So it occurred
) me that, as we're in the same boat, a spot of joint com-
anionship wouldn't come amiss.'

Though she had her doubts about Gray Gallagher being
comfortable companion, perhaps she should take this un-
xpected opportunity. A trip to California might be just what
he needed to enable her to kick-start her life again.

After weeks of being alone and in despair, trapped in a kind of vacuum, it was time she at least made an effort to pick up the pieces and face the future.

As though following her train of thought, Gray pressed 'Short-term at least, we could each fill a gap in the other's life.'

It sounded good, except that the gap in her life was too big to fill, Rebecca thought bleakly.

His green eyes on her face, Gray asked sardonically, 'Or perhaps no one else could *possibly* fill the gap Jason has left?'

Ruffled by the blatant mockery, she answered shortly 'No, they couldn't. But there must be plenty of women in California who'd be only too happy to fill the gap in *your* life. Taking me would be like taking coals to Newcastle.'

'I agree that there are probably plenty of women out there, but I don't want to spend half my holiday looking for one. I just want to take it easy with someone I already know.'

'But we haven't got to know one another yet,' she pointed out.

A devilish gleam in his eye, he said, 'Considering we only met yesterday, I know quite a lot about you.'

Deciding it was safest to let that go, she went on tartly 'And if we did get to know one another, we might find we weren't at all compatible.'

Leering at her, he suggested, 'Alternatively, we might discover that we were strongly attracted... Suppose we couldn't keep our hands off each other?'

Realising that he was teasing her, she made herself say matter-of-factly, 'If it's all the same to you, I'd rather suppose we *could*.'

He grinned appreciatively.

Thinking how attractive he looked when he smiled, she added firmly, 'In all probability, we'd dislike each other.'

'I don't see how you come to that conclusion,' he objected. 'However, if we did happen to discover that we couldn't stand the sight of one another there's no great harm done. It should be relatively easy to behave in a civilised manner for a couple of weeks. Don't you agree?'

She nodded. 'I suppose so.'

'In that case, what do you say?'

Wavering, she asked seriously, 'But won't it affect your arrangements in Boston?'

'Not in the slightest. All I'll have to do is phone ahead and book another room.'

'And you're sure it won't get you into trouble with Philip Lorne?'

'Quite sure.'

Wondering if she could trust him, she hesitated.

'Don't I look harmless enough?'

With that gleam in his eye he looked anything but. Unwilling, for a variety of reasons, to say so, she retorted, 'Crippen *looked* harmless.'

'Well, judged by that yardstick, you'll be quite safe so long as you don't marry me.

'So what do you say?'

'All right.'

'Great.'

He rose and glanced at his watch. 'We haven't a lot of spare time. We'll need to be at the airport in a little under two hours. How long will it take you to pack and find your passport?'

On her feet now, she answered dazedly, 'No more than fifteen minutes.'

'Excellent! Don't forget to put in something warm for the evenings, just in case. Though it will most likely be hot and sunny, northern California isn't exactly the Caribbean.'

When she just continued to stand there, her expression dazed, he queried, 'Is there a problem?'

'I just can't believe I'm actually going to see the west coast.'

Ironically, he said, 'After losing out in the marriage stakes, look on it as a consolation prize. Off you go, now.'

Moving like some automaton, she went into the bedroom, and took a medium-sized suitcase from her cupboard. Her being naturally tidy and organised made it a simple matter to select and pack a small but versatile wardrobe, and she was ready in less than fifteen minutes.

A light woollen coat over her arm, she picked up her bag and case and went through to the living-room to find Gray was standing by the window looking out, his broad back to the room.

She noticed how neatly his ears were set against his well-shaped head, and the way his thick, dark hair, albeit cut short, tried to curl into the nape of his neck.

Though her feet made no sound on the carpet, he turned at her approach.

'Full marks,' he applauded. Then in surprise, 'Is this all the luggage you're taking?'

'Yes.'

Relieving her of the case, and heading for the door, he observed, 'I'm beginning to realise you're a very unusual woman. My ex-girlfriend would have needed at least three suitcases as well as loads of hand luggage.'

'I don't have all that many clothes,' she said.

'Is that from choice or necessity?'

Unwilling to admit that it was from necessity, she said quickly, 'I must just drop my key next door and ask Joanne to do the washing and clear the fridge.'

'What a practical woman you are,' he teased.

'That's why I make a good PA.'

The key delivered, and a hasty promise given to explain everything on her return, Rebecca followed Gray out to the waiting car.

After the previous warm, sunny spell, the weather had turned appreciably cooler. A brisk wind drove a flock of ragged grey clouds across the sky like unruly sheep, and it was beginning to spit with rain.

He put her case in the boot, and, with a courtesy that seemed to come naturally to him, opened the door for her and helped her into the front passenger seat of what she now realised was a sumptuous car.

She should have been high on excitement, she thought as he slid behind the wheel, but instead her mind lay curiously still and empty.

It was as though she had suddenly let go of all her worries about the past and future; as though she had given up trying to control her life, and had simply accepted what was happening to her.

CHAPTER FOUR

THE drive to the airport proved to be a silent one. Gray appeared to be busy with his thoughts, while Rebecca sat staring at the passing scenery without any of it really registering.

On arrival they were met by a nice-looking, efficient young man wearing a smart suit and carrying a clipboard.

'Kevin, how are you?' Gray asked cordially.

'Fine, thank you, Mr Gallagher.'

The two men shook hands.

'This is Miss Ferris, who's been working at our London branch.'

'Nice to meet you, Miss Ferris.'

'Everything under control?' Gray queried, retrieving a laptop from the boot.

'Absolutely. Most of the formalities have been attended to, and take-off should be in forty-five minutes' time. If you'd like to go ahead, I'll see that the rest of your luggage is put on board and the car taken care of.'

Leaving the noise and bustle of the main concourse, they went through to a private lounge, the door of which was guarded by a member of the uniformed security staff.

Squaring his shoulders, the man said respectfully, 'Good morning, Mr Gallagher.'

'Morning…Peters, isn't it?'

'That's right, sir.' He looked gratified, as if remembering his name was a compliment. Then, opening the door, 'Hope you have a good flight, sir, madam.'

'Thanks,' Gray said easily.

Her conviction that Gray Gallagher must be high up in

the company reinforced, she allowed herself to be escorted into an opulent lounge, obviously set apart for VIPs.

A female member of the airport staff, smartly dressed and not a blonde hair out of place, was waiting to welcome them.

'Everything's nicely on schedule, Mr Gallagher. You'll be able to go on board shortly.' Including Rebecca in her smile, she added, 'It should be a nice, smooth flight.'

Having been shown to a blue suede settee, they were served with excellent coffee and petits fours.

Accepting the coffee, Rebecca shook her head at the array of small fancy cakes and biscuits.

'I take it you haven't eaten yet?' Gray queried.

'No. I didn't want anything earlier.'

'You must be starving. If you'd prefer, I'll ask for something plainer. A sandwich perhaps?'

Touched by his concern, she said, 'No, thank you. I'm fine.' Oddly enough, she still wasn't feeling at all hungry.

'Well, if you prefer to wait, we'll have an early lunch on the plane.'

Through the smoked-glass panels of the outer wall she could see a sleek executive jet drawn up quite close by. She thought how tiny it looked in comparison to the huge passenger jets that were coming and going in the distance.

They had just finished their second cup of coffee when the blonde returned to tell them they could board as soon as they were ready.

A hand at her waist, Rebecca found herself escorted across the tarmac and up the steps to the plane, where a steward was waiting to greet them and take their coats. Once they were safely on board, the steps were wheeled away, and the door was closed and locked into place.

As soon as they were seated in the small cabin and their belts fastened, the jet began to taxi to the head of the runway, where, Gray told her, the pilot would go through the last-minute safety checks while he waited for clearance.

'We're off,' he said with satisfaction, when after a few minutes they began to move.

It wasn't until they had started to accelerate that Rebecca lost colour and began to tremble.

Perhaps it was a backlash from her previous, unnatural calm, combined with a lack of food, that conspired to produce a feeling of nausea, followed by a rising panic that threatened to overwhelm her.

She was sitting absolutely still, staring straight ahead, when Gray took her icy cold hand in a warm, comforting clasp.

'It's all right,' he assured her. 'I've taken off and landed countless times and lived to tell the tale. Our pilot, Captain John Connelly, is very experienced. He was flying jumbo jets for one of the top airlines before joining Finance International...'

Holding her hand, he kept talking quietly, reassuring, until they were safely airborne and had levelled out.

'All right now?' he queried.

'Yes... Thank you... I—I'm sorry...'

'There's absolutely no need to be. Feel up to making a move?'

'Yes, of course.'

'Then let me show you around before we eat.'

He lifted her hand and touched his lips to the delicate blue-veined skin on the inside of her wrist, before releasing it.

Her heart gave a queer lurch, and she felt suddenly breathless. Telling herself that it was all part of her previous panic, she unbuckled her seat belt and rose to her feet.

A hand at her waist, he escorted her into an attractive lounge. It was furnished with a bookcase, a businesslike desk and swivel chair, a console incorporating a TV and a music centre, a soft leather couch, two matching armchairs and a coffee-table.

There was a Persian carpet on the floor, and on one

bulkhead a fine modern painting she recognised as a Jonathan Cass.

Putting the laptop on the desk, and following the direction of her gaze, Gray asked, 'Do you like modern art?'

'Some,' she answered cautiously.

'What do you think of Cass?'

'I thought his last exhibition was wonderful. He can get so much *feeling* into his work.'

'Do you have a favourite?'

'*Images.*'

Nodding, as if he was satisfied with her answer, Gray led the way through to the rear of the plane, where there was a shower-room and toilet, and a small, but sumptuous, bedroom.

She had never been inside a privately owned jet before and was staggered by the quiet luxury that surrounded her.

Returning to the lounge, he settled her on the couch and took a seat beside her.

Almost at once there was a discreet knock, and a white-coated steward appeared, and queried, 'Would you care for a pre-lunch drink, sir, madam?'

Turning to Rebecca, Gray raised an enquiring brow.

Repressing a shudder, she shook her head. 'I don't think so, thank you.'

'Just lunch, please, Malcolm.'

'No wine, sir?'

'No wine.'

The steward, small and wiry, with thinning grey hair, returned promptly wheeling a luncheon trolley set with silver cutlery and delicate china.

Having positioned it by the port windows, he drew up a couple of dining chairs.

'We'll serve ourselves,' Gray told him. 'I'll ring when we're ready for coffee.'

'Chef asked me to mention he's made blackcurrant cheesecake, not too sweet, just as you like it.'

'Perhaps you'll thank him, and bring some in with the coffee?'

'Certainly, sir.'

When he had pulled out Rebecca's chair, still standing, Gray lifted the silver lids from the various dishes and told her, 'There are savoury pancakes, asparagus tips, stuffed baby aubergine, baked artichoke hearts and herb dumplings. What would you like?'

Still feeling hollow and queasy, rather than hungry, she began, 'I'm not sure if I—'

'You must eat something,' he broke in firmly. 'You're much too thin as it is…'

When she began to shake her head, he pointed out, 'I've seen you without any clothes, remember, so don't try to tell that's not the case.'

As he watched her blush furiously, he reflected that it was refreshing to find a woman who could still blush. These days a lot of women were far too worldly to be embarrassed by the thought of a strange man seeing them naked.

Finding it a sweet amusement to tease her, he added, 'Though for the sake of *your* ego, I should mention that no man in his right senses would have been disappointed.'

Amber eyes sparkling with anger, she retorted smartly, 'How very kind of you tell me.'

So in spite of the battering she'd taken recently she still had spirit, he decided admiringly.

'Though it really wasn't necessary,' she went on, '*my* ego's fine.' And thought, *if only that were true*.

'I must say I'm glad to hear it,' he said smoothly. Then with genuine regret, 'Sorry if I sounded patronising. It wasn't intentional.'

Stony-faced, she muttered, 'I bet.'

'Truly.'

She found it hard to believe that this man would do or say anything that wasn't intentional. He had too much *awareness*, too much self-control.

Looking at her from beneath absurdly long lashes, he coaxed, 'Pax?'

Suddenly finding him extremely likeable, she smiled and answered, 'Pax.'

Rocked by the radiance of that smile, and wondering how he could ever have thought her less than beautiful, he stooped and touched his lips to hers.

Taken completely by surprise, the shock of that lightest of kisses sent her heart racing and stopped her breath. After a moment she asked huskily, 'What did you do that for?'

His face innocent, as if he had no idea of the havoc that brief meeting of mouths had caused, he said, 'It seemed appropriate. Surely pax is the kiss of peace?'

Then prosaically, 'Now, suppose I give you a pancake and some asparagus? You should enjoy them both. Henri is an excellent chef.'

After she had forced down the first mouthful or two, her empty stomach settled and she began to eat with an appetite.

'That's more like it,' Gray approved, and helped her to another pancake before tucking into his own.

She hadn't expected to eat it all, but somehow she did, and even managed a piece of cheesecake.

When the steward tapped and came in to wheel away the lunch trolley, they moved to the couch to drink their second cup of coffee.

'How do you feel now you've eaten?' Gray queried.

'Much better, thank you.'

'You've got a bit more colour. It's my guess that for a long time now you haven't been either eating or sleeping properly. Jason has a lot to answer for.'

Rebecca shook her head. 'It's not fair to blame Jason. It isn't his fault.'

'Then who would you blame?'

'Nobody, really.'

'Not even Lisa?'

'She couldn't have taken him if he hadn't wanted to go,' Rebecca said evenly.

'How very philosophical.'

'Nor could she have made him marry her if he hadn't wanted to.'

'That's not necessarily true. Believe me, there are ways and means. Though at his age, Jason should have known better than to fall for any of them.'

His voice exasperated, Gray added, 'He can be a complete and utter fool at times.'

'I suppose he couldn't help the way he felt about Lisa, any more than he could help the way I felt about him.'

'Are you trying to tell me that as far as you were concerned he didn't make the first move? That *you* made all the running?'

'No, of course not, but—'

'So *he* did?'

'Well, yes…'

'Which means he wanted you?'

'I thought he did,' she said hesitantly.

'I'm *sure* he did. At least physically. But from what you've told me, he wasn't getting very far.

'Whereas most women would have been only too happy to move in with him, he'd been unable to persuade you to. Which must have aggravated him enormously.'

When she remained silent, Gray went on, 'Despite his charm, Jason can be surprisingly ruthless. He'll go to almost any lengths to get what he wants, as was made evident by his previous engagements.'

'I don't understand.'

Patiently, he explained, 'Apart from the two he admitted to, I happen to know that if some bit of fluff he particularly lusted after was holding out on him, he'd produce an engagement ring.

'Then when he got tired of her, or someone new came

along, he'd tell "his fiancée" regretfully that it had been a mistake.

'If she showed any signs of playing up, he'd offer to let her keep the ring. When it comes to the crunch, most women will settle for what they can get,' Gray added cynically.

Angrily, she asked, 'Are you saying that Jason regarded me as just another bit of fluff?'

'You don't believe he did?'

'No, I don't!' She didn't *want* to believe it. She *wouldn't* believe it.

'Well, whether you believe it or not, Jason's behaviour leaves a lot to be desired. He's obviously caused you a lot of heartache and brought you down.'

'Jason isn't to blame,' she said again. 'My father's sudden death had come as a shock, and I was feeling very low when we met.

'That's what made meeting him so special and wonderful—' She stopped speaking abruptly.

Gray's mouth tightened, but all he said was, 'You must have missed your father a good deal.'

'I loved him dearly, and he was the only person who had ever really cared about me,' she said simply.

'He couldn't have been all that old; what did he die of?'

'A series of heart attacks.' Her voice shook a little. 'He was only forty-nine. But things hadn't been going well for some time. He'd had a great deal of stress. A lot of financial problems to cope with.

'The company's profits had been falling steadily over a number of years. Then when one big deal went disastrously wrong, Bowman Ferris lost a huge amount of money.

'In order to survive, Dad was forced to mortgage Elmslee. From then on things went from bad to worse. He did his best to hide it, but I knew he was having a desperate struggle.'

'So that's why you refused an allowance?'

'I didn't want an allowance.'

'Which I suppose, in the circumstances, was just as well,' Gray commented, frowning.

Suspecting a hint of censure, she hurried to her father's defence. 'Elmslee has never been cheap to maintain, Lisa was at an expensive boarding-school, and Helen too used to a life of luxury to cut down on her spending—'

'While you went out to work.'

'I *wanted* to,' she insisted. 'If we'd still been well off, I would have done the same...'

Gray said nothing, but she could sense his anger.

'None of it was my father's fault. He did his very best. Though Bowman Ferris was on the verge of bankruptcy when Dad died and Finance International took over, he'd made a deal to ensure there was enough money to continue to pay the mortgage on Elmslee, and also to provide Helen with a modest personal allowance.'

'A bit hand-to-mouth when someone's used to spending freely,' Gray commented. 'Which is no doubt why she decided to sell the manor.'

'Dad did his utmost to protect his family and Elmslee,' Rebecca said again.

'But while Helen would presumably take care of Lisa, he'd made no provision for you.'

'You knew how things were?'

'Yes, I knew.'

Being one of Finance International's top executives, of course he would know.

Her voice hoarse, she said, 'And that was why you suspected me of trying to marry Jason for his money!'

He made no attempt to refute the charge. 'I must admit that I did at first, but it—'

'I hate you!' she burst out.

Taking her hand, which was clenched into a tight fist, he said with infuriating calmness, 'There's no reason to get upset.'

'I think there's every reason.'

She tried to pull her hand free, but, refusing to release it, he began to straighten her fingers one at a time, kissing each one as he did so. 'If you let me finish what I was saying…'

Knowing it was childish, but unable to prevent herself, she turned her head away.

'Are you listening?' he enquired silkily.

When she didn't answer he put the tip of her index finger in his mouth and sucked.

Shivers running up and down her spine, she croaked, 'I'm listening.'

'I was about to say that it didn't take me long to realise I was mistaken.' Then, gently, 'If you look at me, I might even apologise.'

Turning to look at him, she met his gaze and held it, even though she could feel her colour rising. 'Go ahead,' she invited, 'apologise.'

'I'm sorry.'

'You don't look a bit sorry.'

He laughed. *'Touché.'*

Then, his eyes fixed on her mouth in a way that made butterflies dance in her stomach, he asked, 'Now what would you like to do?'

'Do?' she echoed.

'For entertainment, I mean. There's a good selection of music, plenty of books, and a wide range of films.'

His eyes gleaming green as any cat's between dense lashes, he added hopefully, 'Or perhaps you'd like to join the—'

'No, I wouldn't!' she broke in sharply, remembering the luxurious bedroom, with its double bed and the coverlet turned down ready.

Face straight, eyes dancing with suppressed laughter, he asked, 'Sure?'

'Quite sure.'

He sighed. 'Oh, well, if you don't fancy the idea… But I thought you might find it interesting to join Captain

Connelly in the cockpit for a while. Enjoy a bird's-eye view of flying.'

'Oh…'

Stroking a fingertip down her hot cheek, he asked, 'Or did you think I meant something else?'

'No, of course not,' she denied hurriedly.

He clicked his tongue in reproof. 'How can you lie like that? You thought I meant the Mile-High Club.'

'That's what you *intended* me to think,' she burst out indignantly. 'And don't bother to deny it!'

'I promise I won't even try.'

'I wish you'd promise to stop teasing me!'

'I'm afraid I can't. I find it almost irresistible. You rise to the bait so nicely…

'By the way, if you want to change your mind…'

'About what?' she asked cautiously.

'Going into the cockpit…'

Knowing it might be the only chance she would ever get, she said, 'I would like to take a look.'

Captain John Connelly, a nice-looking, middle-aged man with iron-grey hair and bushy eyebrows, greeted their entrance with equanimity.

'Good to see you, Mr Gallagher.'

'Nice to see you, John.'

Leaning negligently against the cockpit door, he made the introduction. 'This is Miss Ferris, who has been working at our London branch.'

'Pleased to meet you, Miss Ferris.' Indicating the co-pilot's seat, he added, 'Take a pew.'

'Thank you.' Feeling a little strange, she eased herself into the seat, and looked through the cockpit window. All she could see ahead was clear, uninterrupted blue, while beneath them a few white cotton-wool clouds floated serenely.

'How's it going?' Gray asked.

Captain Connelly made an O with his thumb and index

finger. 'Flying conditions are excellent. We should be in Boston well on time. Would you like to take over for a while?'

So Gray was a pilot too, Rebecca thought. Then wondered why she was surprised. Already she felt sure that he was the kind of man who could do or be anything he chose.

'No, thanks, I've some work to catch up on,' he answered easily. 'But first I thought Miss Ferris might like some idea of how you fly a jet.'

'To be absolutely honest, this thing virtually flies itself...'

While Rebecca listened with unfeigned interest, Captain Connelly explained how the aircraft's controls worked and what the various instruments and gauges were for.

'Piloting a plane must be stimulating,' she remarked at length.

'Admittedly it's never dull, but like any other job it becomes routine after a time.'

When they had chatted for a while, in spite of finding it all fascinating, Rebecca was forced to smother a yawn.

Gray, who seemed to miss nothing, asked, 'About ready to make a move?'

'Yes.'

'Thanks, John,' he addressed the pilot. 'We'll leave you to it.'

Rising to her feet, Rebecca added her thanks to Gray's before following him from the cockpit.

'You look tired,' he remarked as they made their way aft.

'I am tired,' she admitted, feeling as though she could sleep for a week.

'Well, as you know there's a perfectly good bed, and it will be several hours yet before we land at Boston. In fact having a nap might not be a bad idea. It'll certainly help with the time difference.'

'Then I will, if you don't mind.'

'Not at all. When I've caught up on some work, I might even...' He paused.

When, remembering his remark about her rising to the bait, she studiously ignored his attempt to tease her, he went on, 'Take a short nap myself. But don't worry, the couch is quite comfortable.'

He gave her a come-hither look. 'Unless you should change your mind about joining a fairly exclusive club. If you do, just let me know.'

Smiling, she answered serenely, 'Thanks, but I won't change my mind.'

'You're learning.' He sounded regretful.

In the bedroom, finding the blinds were already pulled down over the windows to keep out the light, Rebecca stripped off to her undies, and, stretching out on the bed, pulled up the lightweight cover.

She barely had time to register that the bed and the pillows were the essence of comfort, before she was fast asleep.

Something touching her cheek made her stir. She put up a hand to brush it away, and, encountering another hand, opened her eyes.

Gray was standing by the bed, smiling down at her.

'Feeling better?'

Her sleep had been sweet and dreamless, and for the first time in weeks she felt completely refreshed.

'Much better, thank you.' Peering at her watch, she exclaimed, 'No wonder! I've slept for hours.'

'You must have needed to. Now, how about a nice cup of tea?'

On the bedside table was a tray set with fine china tea things and a plate of biscuits.

'Sounds wonderful.' Pushing herself into a sitting position, she dragged the coverlet up with her and trapped it under her arms.

Appearing amused by her modesty, he reached for the teapot. 'Milk and sugar?'

'Just milk, please.'

Noticing there were two cups and saucers, she asked, 'Are you joining me?'

'Are you inviting me to?'

'What if I say no?'

'Then I'll take mine in the lounge,' he answered cheerfully, and, filling two cups, handed her one.

'Thank you.'

He waited.

She held her breath while she counted to ten.

Picking up his own cup, he was about to turn away, when she asked demurely, 'Please won't you join me?'

His green eyes gleaming, he sat down on the edge of the bed and turned to face her.

Suddenly he was much too close for comfort. She could feel his muscular thigh pressing against her leg through the thin coverlet.

Heat rose in her body, and her heart began to race in the most disconcerting manner.

She was trying to ease her leg away a fraction without making it obvious, when he queried silkily, 'I'm not crowding you, I trust?'

Realising too late that she couldn't hope to win, and wishing she hadn't deliberately set out to tease him, she fought back, 'No, not at all.'

His ironic little salute acknowledged a worthy opponent, before he observed, 'We'll be landing at Logan Airport in about twenty minutes, so I'm afraid there's no time to continue our game.'

With a feeling of relief, she said, 'Then we'll call it a draw, shall we?'

'Not at all,' he disagreed, and, taking her hand, kissed the palm.

Her stomach plunged as though she'd stepped off a very high building.

'I've found it most entertaining,' he added, 'and I look forward to resuming later.'

She could only hope that either he didn't mean it, or when 'later' came he would have forgotten all about it.

Logan International Airport was only three miles from the centre of Boston, and, coming in to land in fine, sunny weather they had an excellent view of the city built on the peninsula formed by the Charles river and Fort Point Channel.

'It looks fantastic,' Rebecca exclaimed.

'You've never been to Boston before?'

She shook her head.

'Do you know much about it?' he queried.

'Only what every schoolgirl remembers, that the seaport was founded by the Puritans in 1630 and outpaced its rivals to become the largest British settlement. Apart from that one bit of history, very little. I suppose you know it well?'

'Fairly well.'

'And you like it?'

'Yes, it's a fascinating mixture of colonial and cosmopolitan, history and high-tech.

'On one hand, up-to-the-minute expressways carry endless streams of traffic, while on the other, the narrow cobblestoned streets of Beacon Hill have a picturesque, turn-of-the-last-century look and feel.'

'It sounds charming. I'd love to see it.'

'When we've checked into our hotel and got rid of the luggage, I'll be happy to show you around.'

Peering from the plane window, she asked, 'Whereabouts are we staying?'

'At the Faneuil, which is in downtown Boston,' Gray told her. Adding humorously, 'The streets there are a driver's nightmare. Rather than following the usual grid system, they appear to have been laid out by the colonial cattle...'

When their taxi drew up outside the Faneuil—a period hotel with a handsome façade—a short, dapper man with dark hair and glasses appeared.

'Mr Gallagher, how nice to have you back.'

'Thanks, Benson. Nice to be back.'

'If you'll come this way, sir, madam.'

A single snap of his fingers summoned a bellboy, smartly uniformed in red and gold, who collected their luggage and followed the little party at a respectful distance.

They took the lift up to the second floor, where, having crossed an inner lobby, the manager opened one of the doors with a flourish.

'As you requested, you have a suite of rooms overlooking the garden—a central sitting-room with a bedroom and bathroom either side...'

Correctly interpreting Rebecca's quick glance, Gray whispered in her ear, 'Don't worry, you can always keep yours locked at night.'

When he'd shown them round, murmuring, 'I hope your stay, short as it is, will be a pleasant one,' Benson bowed himself out.

After the bellboy had deposited their luggage, pocketed a handsome tip and departed, Gray turned to Rebecca and suggested, 'If you want to freshen up, I'll give you a knock in about ten minutes, shall I?'

She nodded. 'Please.'

He disappeared into his own bedroom, closing the communicating door quietly behind him.

Rebecca followed suit, and, glancing around at the understated but evident luxury, wondered uneasily how much all this was costing and who would be picking up the bill.

Finance International presumably. She only hoped Philip Lorne never got to hear about it.

She had just washed her face and hands and unpacked what she thought she might need for the night, when the knock came.

'How are you doing?' Gray's voice enquired.

She opened the door. 'All ready.'

'In that case, let's go.' He sounded so full of *joie de vivre* that she felt her spirits rise.

He had changed his short coat for a well-cut leather jacket and looked both elegant and sexy.

'There's a bistro just round the corner, so I suggest we have a bite to eat first.'

Suddenly finding she was hungry, she agreed, 'That sounds great.'

'Like French food?'

'Love it. Apart from snails and oysters, that is.'

'I can agree as far as snails go, and I admit to preferring my oysters smoked.'

La Renaissance looked fairly ordinary, with narrow, high-backed booths and an unpretentious decor. But Rebecca soon found that the food, though simple, was out of this world.

As, sitting side by side, they ate bowls of thick garbure blanche, he asked, 'So what would you like to see, apart from Beacon Hill?'

'Will we have time for anything else? I thought you had a business appointment?'

'It's a business dinner, to be precise, scheduled for eight o'clock at the Faneuil.' He stopped speaking as the waiter came to take away their bowls, and serve iced glasses of coupe martuxa.

The raspberry sundaes were delicious, and Rebecca had almost finished hers, when she noticed that Gray's eyes were fixed on her mouth in a way that made her toes curl.

His intention was clear, but before she could do anything to deflect it, he leaned towards her and licked the corner of her mouth.

Though it was over in a split-second, the erotic little gesture transfixed her. It was as openly sexy as if he'd reached across and unbuttoned her blouse.

As she sat quite still, her spoon poised in mid-air, he explained, 'A tiny flake of raspberry.'

Then, as though nothing untoward had happened, he ordered coffee and calmly turned the conversation back to sightseeing.

'When we've had a look at Beacon Hill, if you're up to walking four kilometres, we could follow the Freedom Trail.'

Still struggling to regain her equilibrium, she asked huskily, 'The Freedom Trail?'

'It's marked by a red line that runs along the city's sidewalks and links sixteen important sites in the history of Boston and America. One of the best known is Paul Revere's house, the oldest in the city. There's also a statue—the Ride of Paul Revere.'

'Of course! We were taught about his famous midnight ride to warn his fellow revolutionaries of the approach of British troops from Boston.'

He smiled at her, a slow smile that started in his eyes before it reached his lips. 'There you are, that's another piece of history you remember.'

Gray, she soon discovered, was an interesting and stimulating companion, and the afternoon proved to be most pleasurable. She loved the old-world charm and atmosphere of Beacon Hill, and the narrow, cobblestoned streets, gas-lit at night, that ran down to the river.

When they had stopped for a rest and a pot of tea in a very English-looking tearoom, they joined the Freedom Trail at Boston Common.

From there they walked to the harbour, where they went on board the frigate *U.S.S. Constitution*, known affectionately as 'Old Ironsides', after British cannon-balls bounced off her heavily planked sides.

When they reached the Bunker Hill Monument, which was the end of the trail, seeing she was getting weary, Gray suggested a taxi back.

It had turned seven when they reached the hotel, and Rebecca, who was starting to think longingly of bed, thanked her lucky stars that she had had such a good sleep on the plane.

They had just reached their suite when, watching her stifle a yawn, Gray asked, 'Tired?'

'I won't be sorry when it's bedtime,' she admitted.

'Well, we shouldn't be too late. Our man's a stickler for punctuality, so with a bit of luck dinner will be over by nine-thirty.'

He sounded as if he was expecting her to join him.

Carefully, she said, 'As you have an appointment, I'd be quite happy to skip dinner and go straight to bed now.'

Gray shook his head decidedly. 'I'd like you to be there too.'

'But surely if it's business…'

'The man I'm meeting prefers his business dealings to take place in a social atmosphere. And as he gets on better with women than with men—most men hate his guts, but women seem to go for his kind of macho charm—he invariably brings a female companion along and expects his opposite number to do the same.'

She recalled one of Jason's business contacts who had worked in much the same way.

'If you hadn't been here I would have had to go to an agency and hire a dinner companion. Which is far from ideal when business is being discussed and things may get heated.'

'You seem to be expecting problems.'

'I am,' Gray admitted ruefully. 'Considering everything, our last meeting went very smoothly. This one, however, promises to be a rough ride.

'Though he's one of the richest men in America he hates to lose money. Over the past six months he's lost quite a lot, and stands to lose more, but somehow I have to convince him that the only way to go is forward.

'If he decides to pull out of the project at this stage, and we can't meet the shortfall, the whole thing will come tumbling round our ears. It'll cost PLFI hundreds of millions of dollars.'

'It won't...?'

'No, it won't bring the company down, but it will be quite a serious blow, and affect several other big investment schemes.'

She was just about to ask him what the project was, when, glancing at his watch, he said, 'We'd better get moving. Can you be ready by a quarter to eight?'

'Yes, of course.'

He grinned. 'Then I'd better go get my spurs buckled on.'

CHAPTER FIVE

SHOWERED and made-up with care, her ash-brown hair swirled into a sleek chignon, Rebecca put on a pair of strappy sandals and a simple, sleeveless sheath, as yet unworn.

Cut with an uneven hemline, its silk chiffon was a swirl of subtle colours over a plain underslip with a built-in bra. Thin slivers of each colour made up the spaghetti shoulder straps.

It was a romantic dress, bought especially for a gala concert Jason had been going to take her to.

She waited for the thought to hurt, but somehow it didn't. Perhaps she had suffered so much pain that she'd grown too numb to feel?

A last quick check in the long mirror, and she was ready with five minutes to spare. Even so, Gray was already in the lounge, sitting at the small desk, his laptop open in front of him.

Glancing up at her approach, he switched off the computer and rose to greet her. His gaze swept over her from head to toe, taking in the glossy hair, the pretty dress and the long, slender legs.

'Will I do?' she asked a shade nervously.

'You look absolutely delightful.' He came over and took her hand.

At five feet eight inches she was tall for a woman, but even though she was wearing high heels Gray was a good six inches taller.

Wearing an evening jacket and a black bow tie, he looked so powerfully attractive that she found herself absurdly breathless.

'It's a great pity we're not free to go out and paint the town,' he said with a rueful smile. 'If this meeting wasn't so important…'

Feeling an odd little flutter, she withdrew her hand and said quickly, 'But it is.'

He sighed. 'I'm afraid so. Right, let's go.'

The hotel restaurant was fairly busy and there was a buzz of talk and laughter as the *maître d'* showed them to one of the more secluded tables.

As soon as they were seated a wine waiter appeared with an ice bucket containing a bottle of vintage champagne, and four long-stemmed glasses.

'Would you like me to open it now, sir?'

'No, thanks, leave it until our guests arrive.'

'Very good, sir.'

A few moments later, glancing up, Gray said softly, 'There they are.'

In the entrance was a tall, heavily built man with grizzled hair that, brushed straight back from his forehead, lay close to his head in tight waves.

By his side was a voluptuous blonde, perhaps half his age. She was wearing a glittering blue dress that left very little to the imagination.

'Just as I expected,' Gray murmured softly. 'A real Barbie doll.'

Rebecca scarcely heard. Her startled gaze was fixed on the man, rather than his companion. But surely it couldn't be…? Though hadn't Jason mentioned that Andrew Scrivener lived in Boston?

As the *maître d'* led them over, her worst fears were confirmed. Though it was a while since she had seen him, there was no mistaking that powerful face with its large, hooked nose and sensual mouth, those obsidian eyes set deep beneath almost black brows.

Gray rose to his feet to greet them, and the two men

shook hands with a show of civility rather than any great cordiality.

To Rebecca's relief, Gray introduced her simply as Miss Ferris, without naming any connection with Finance International.

Hoping for the best, she held her breath.

Andrew Scrivener acknowledged her courteously, but, though his hooded eyes lingered on her face for longer than was necessary, he made no mention of them having met before.

For which she was truly thankful.

When the introductions had been completed, Gray suggested, 'Perhaps you'd like to eat first and discuss business later?'

'Fine by me,' Scrivener agreed.

Gray signalled the waiter and, apart from Rebecca, who asked for mineral water, they drank champagne while they looked at the menu and gave their order.

That done, while the blonde, whose name was Marianne Midler, stared around her, Gray chose a safe topic of conversation and made a determined effort to break the ice.

He was getting very little response from Scrivener, when, remembering something she had learnt from Jason, Rebecca mentioned the arts.

'I understand that Symphony Hall houses both the Boston Symphony and the Boston Pops Orchestras?'

His heavy face suddenly becoming animated, Scrivener asked, 'Indeed it does. You like music, Miss Ferris?'

'Yes, very much.'

'Have you ever been to Symphony Hall?'

'No, I haven't. This is my first trip to Boston.'

'How long are you here for?'

'Just one night.'

'Pity.'

With a glance at Gray, he asked, 'I can't persuade you to stay on?'

'I'm afraid not. We're due to fly out to California tomorrow afternoon.'

'I'm heading that way myself in a week or so to see how my new house is progressing. Then I'll be visiting my younger sister in San Francisco. She's just given birth to her second child, so we've cause to celebrate.'

The blonde shuddered. 'I'd *hate* to be pregnant.'

Scrivener gave her a cold look.

'I just bet you feel the same.' She appealed to Rebecca for help.

'I'm afraid not,' Rebecca said evenly. 'If I ever get married I'd like a family.'

'But think what having a baby does to your figure!'

'It's just as well all women aren't like you,' Scrivener observed, frowning.

Putting a hand on his sleeve, the nails painted a shimmering blue to match her dress, she protested, 'But Andy, darling—'

'Stow it, Marianne,' he said curtly.

As, pouting prettily, she withdrew her hand he turned his attention back to Gray. 'It's a business trip, I take it?'

'Partly. Finance International have acquired the Santa Rosa vineyard in the Napa Valley, so I'm going to take a look at the prospects.'

'Ought to be good. We're practically neighbours. A few years back I bought Hillsden Wineries and put in an experienced manager.

'Though Collins is only young he certainly knows his stuff, and since then it's been going from strength to strength. Choose the right manager, and yours should do the same.'

Turning to Rebecca and sounding almost jovial, Scrivener said, 'Well, if you can't stay right now, you must certainly come to Boston again. During the summer there are open-air concerts down by the river.

'Marianne likes music…don't you, babe?'

Basking in the renewed warmth of his attention, the blonde changed her pout to a smile, and from then on the atmosphere became more relaxed and the conversation flowed easily.

Andrew Scrivener, as Rebecca recalled, had a certain charm when he chose to use it, and during an excellent meal he showed a side of himself that could only be described as charismatic.

Coffee and liqueurs had been served and drunk before business was mentioned. Then the atmosphere abruptly changed for the worse as the two men embarked on a low-toned discussion that, on Scrivener's part at least, sounded distinctly irate.

Apparently bored by business matters, Marianne claimed Rebecca's attention and launched into a monologue on her last cosmetic surgery, and what she was planning to 'improve' next. 'I thought I might have my bottom lip made fuller...'

While Rebecca did her best to look like an interested listener, more than half her attention was focused on what the men were saying.

But with Marianne's strident voice tending to drown out the other conversation, all she could pick out were odd, disjointed phrases.

It seemed to be a battle royal. But while Gray stayed cool and firm, but restrained, Scrivener got even more heated and hostile.

After a while it became obvious that Gray was fighting a losing battle, as the other man refused to listen to him.

'You're wasting your time, Gallagher. I'm pulling out as of now.'

When Marianne paused for breath, Rebecca heard him add angrily, 'I was a fool to get involved in the first place. If I'd played my hunch and taken notice of Miss Ferris instead of young Beaumont...'

She froze. So he *did* remember her!

Gray looked up sharply. 'I wasn't aware that you and Miss Ferris had met.'

'Beaumont brought her along to that first meeting in London and introduced her as his PA. If I remember rightly, you were in the Middle East at the time; that's why he was standing in for you.

'He's a bit of a lightweight, and still wet behind the ears in some ways. It's a pity I ever agreed to meet him. His review of the situation wasn't sound.'

Coolly, Gray suggested, 'Perhaps you'd like to tell me exactly what was said?'

'He said that the then current backers of the Archangel Project had gone broke and it was a good chance to get in on the ground floor.

'I pointed out that the complex had so far failed dismally to attract customers.

'He argued that, though it had got off to a bad start, it was still a sound financial bet, and being able to buy into it at such a late stage was an opportunity not to be missed.

'I ought to have waited and talked to you,' he added in disgust.

'If you had, I would have told you exactly the same. When the whole project is really up and running it will be worth billions.'

'In my opinion it'll never be up and running. It's just one big white elephant. When you think about it, who the hell would want to holiday in a series of huge plastic domes in the middle of a desert?'

'With the facilities they'll offer when completed, my guess would be quite a lot of people.'

Scrivener shook his head. 'Wishful thinking. My gut says the whole complex will probably just sit there and rot.

'When I'm doing business, I tend to follow my hunches. At that meeting in London, though I had a hunch Miss Ferris was right, I didn't follow it.'

Gray frowned. 'I don't quite see how Miss Ferris comes into this.'

'I asked her what she honestly thought of the Archangel Project.

'When, obviously unwilling to follow Beaumont's lead, she tried to sidestep the question, I asked if she would invest any of her own money in the project.

'She said no, she couldn't help but feel it was too big a risk.

'I've always been impressed by a woman's ability to use her intuition, especially when that intuition goes hand in hand with a sound grasp of business and a good brain. I believe Miss Ferris has both. I also admire her integrity.'

Turning to Rebecca, he went on, 'My hunch told me you were right, and I should have listened.'

She took a deep breath, and said firmly, 'I'm extremely glad you didn't, Mr Scrivener, because now I'm convinced I made a mistake.'

His black eyes boring into her, he sneered, 'So this time, instead of being totally honest, you're saying what Gallagher's instructed you to say.'

'I'm doing nothing of the kind. Mr Gallagher never instructed me to say anything. I didn't even know who he was meeting until you came into the restaurant.'

Scrivener shook his head. 'Miss Ferris, I'm disappointed in you. Presumably you've moved up the ladder and are now Gallagher's PA, so—'

'But I'm not. I no longer work for PLFI.' Lifting her chin, she added, 'And if I did, I still wouldn't be prepared to say anything I didn't believe.'

Watching him weigh up her words, she added, 'When I said I personally wouldn't put money into the Archangel Project, it was because at that point I thought it had been built in the wrong place at the wrong time.

'Since then I've revised that opinion. After all, Las Vegas

started out in the middle of a desert. And on that showing, Archangel could be the holiday place of the future.'

'*Could* be?'

'I was being cautious. I'm sure it *will* be.'

'So are you saying I should go on?' His harsh voice held a challenge.

'It's not my place to say any such thing, but I certainly believe it's the best option by far.

'For one thing, if you pull out now you must stand to lose everything you've already put into it, which would be a terrible waste.'

'If I go on, I could lose a whole lot more.'

'You *could*,' Gray took up the baton, 'but the last report I saw made me believe that most of the teething troubles are over and that things are starting to run more smoothly.

'I'm not suggesting that there won't be some ups and downs, and maybe it won't start to make money for a year or two yet, but all the signs are there that when it does take off, it'll take off big.'

'And you agree?' Scrivener asked Rebecca.

'I'm convinced it will become a millionaire's playground.' She smiled at him mischievously. 'You may even want to holiday there yourself.'

For a moment he appeared amused by her audacity, then, his eyes glittering like a snake's, he asked, 'If you're no longer working for PLFI, what are you doing here in Boston with Gallagher?'

Ambushed by the question, and aware that if she looked at Gray for guidance Andrew Scrivener would think the worst, she hesitated. Then after a moment, seeing nothing else for it, she answered with as much sang-froid as she could muster, 'As it happens I'm with Mr Gallagher for purely personal reasons.'

Those hooded eyes pinned her. 'Personal reasons?'

'Miss Ferris is taking a holiday in California as my guest,' Gray told him levelly.

'I see…' Scrivener's sensual lips twisted. 'Well, I must say I envy you, having such a charming and *loyal* companion.'

Before Gray could make any answer, Rebecca said crisply, 'If you think my loyalty stretches to lying, then you're quite wrong.'

Sounding unimpressed, Scrivener remarked, 'I believe that most women would lie for a man they're in love with.'

'You may be right, but—'

'Are you trying to tell me you're different?'

'No. I'm trying to tell you that it isn't what you seem to imagine. The relationship between myself and Mr Gallagher is quite platonic. I'm certainly *not* in love with him.'

His powerful head tilted a little to one side, he surveyed her. 'You have the look of a woman in love.'

When, suddenly rattled, she failed to deny it, he said, 'Is it because of young Beaumont?'

'How did you know?'

'I remember the way you looked at him. I must admit I quite envied him. So perhaps you're toeing the company line to keep *him* in a job?'

'Did I toe it last time?'

'No, and, judging by the look on his face, he wasn't at all pleased.'

'No, he wasn't.'

In fact Jason had been furious with her for speaking her mind, and later they had had their one and only row.

'Why the devil didn't you back me up,' he had demanded angrily, 'instead of nearly scuppering the whole deal? You must surely have realised that PLFI couldn't afford to go it alone, that we need Scrivener's cooperation.'

'I'm sorry Mr Scrivener asked for my opinion. I wish he hadn't. But I wasn't prepared to lie to him and tell him I thought the Archangel was a good bet when I don't believe it is.

'The last lot of investors to pull out were the third, and

most of them have ended up bankrupt. That project just swallows money, and so many things have gone wrong that it seems to me to be jinxed.'

'Well, it's a damned good job he listened to me and not to you, or I'd have had Uncle Pip down on me like a ton of bricks.'

After a few days he had ostensibly forgiven her, but he never again suggested she accompany him to any business meetings.

'But presumably he forgave you?' Scrivener's voice broke into her thoughts.

'Yes, of course,' she answered evenly.

'Who could do anything else?' he remarked with ponderous gallantry. Then pointedly, 'So if all's well, why are you going on holiday with Gallagher, rather than Beaumont?'

Wanting to say, *mind your own business*, but unwilling to lose any advantage they might have gained, she told him flatly, 'Because yesterday Jason married my sister, and today they're off on their honeymoon. That's the reason I felt forced to leave Finance International.'

Hearing the catch in her voice, Gray jumped in. 'We were sorry to lose Miss Ferris, who, as you remarked earlier, has both a sound grasp of business and a good brain. I felt that at the very least the company owed her a holiday.'

'I see.'

From his expression it was impossible to tell whether or not he believed what he had been told.

Glancing at Marianne, who hadn't said a word while the little drama was being played out, Scrivener stood up. 'Well, it's time we were going. Thanks for the meal, Gallagher.'

Gray rose to his feet and, having pulled out the blonde's chair, wished her a pleasant, 'Goodnight, Miss Midler.'

As the two men shook hands, Scrivener said, 'I'll let you know my final decision some time tomorrow.'

'We'll be starting for California mid-afternoon.'

'I'll catch you on your mobile. I have the number.' Then to Rebecca, 'It was nice meeting you again, Miss Ferris. I hope you have an enjoyable holiday.'

'Thank you.'

Watching the two walk away, she felt suddenly cold and wrung out, on the point of exhaustion.

Resuming his seat, Gray said exultantly, 'You were absolutely wonderful, and the company is very much in your debt.'

Rebecca felt a glow of returning warmth at his unstinting praise. She had wondered a little uneasily if he might have been annoyed by her involvement.

Watching her cheeks take on a tinge of colour, he queried, 'I presume Jason has been keeping tabs on the Archangel Project?'

'Not as far as I know. I just happened to see a well-informed article by James Berringer, the *Globe*'s financial correspondent.

'He presented the facts, then went on to look ahead and compare Archangel with other futuristic projects that in the end proved wildly successful. After a lot of thought, I revised my earlier opinion.'

'Thank the lord you did. If I *had* primed you, I think Scrivener would have known. But as it was, you came over as totally convinced and convincing, the only combination that could have tipped the scales in our favour.'

He leaned forward and, taking her face between his palms, kissed her on the mouth.

A jubilant kiss that held both relief and satisfaction; an ardent kiss that had her trembling and confused.

For the briefest of kisses in a public place it sent out shockwaves that rocked her very being, and triggered a sudden and overwhelming hunger.

She knew without a shadow of doubt that not even Jason's kisses had affected her so powerfully. If they had, she would never have found the strength to hold out against him.

Drawing back, Gray went on, 'Scrivener came absolutely determined to withdraw from the project, and you managed to achieve what I would have found impossible had I been on my own.'

Noticing that his voice had roughened somewhat and his face looked taut, as though the skin had been stretched too tightly over the bones, she said breathlessly, 'He may still withdraw.'

'I very much doubt it. I know him well enough to be sure that if he'd still been determined to pull out, he would have said so at once.'

Then, as though making an effort to return to normal, 'Now, shall we relax for a little while? You didn't have a brandy earlier, and you've more than earned one.'

She shook her head. 'I don't really care for brandy. But I would like some more coffee.'

'Sure it won't keep you awake?'

'I doubt if anything could do that.'

'Yes, you must be shattered. I'm afraid we're somewhat later than I'd expected. It'll be the early hours of the morning in London.'

'Well, at least I had some sleep on the plane.'

'Even so, you look about all in.'

They were making polite conversation like two strangers, while beneath the surface a silent and much deeper communication was going on, telling of need and hunger, of excitement and anticipation.

Reaching across the table, he took hold of her wrist. Her pulse beneath the light pressure of his thumb was rapid and uneven, and as she looked up he saw that her golden eyes appeared slightly dazed, their pupils large and dark.

Moving his thumb to stroke her palm, he suggested, 'It might make more sense to go straight up to our suite and have coffee served there.'

When she made no objection he rose to pull out her chair, and a hand at her waist escorted her out of the restaurant.

She was acutely conscious of his height, the length of his stride, the sexual tension between them.

The lift had just gone up to the top floor, and by tacit consent they used the stairs. They climbed in silence, without looking at one another, but from time to time her elbow touched his, or their thighs brushed lightly.

Outwardly they must have looked like any ordinary couple, but she was so aware of him that she found it difficult to breathe, and her heart was beating in great heavy thuds, so that she felt sure he must be able to hear it pounding.

When they reached their suite he opened the door with no sign of haste, and, having followed her inside, set his back to the panels.

He hadn't bothered to switch on the light, and in the glow of the city's not-quite-darkness she turned towards him.

Without a single word being spoken, he took her in his arms and began to kiss her as no one had ever kissed her before, or ever would again.

Kisses that went on and on, blowing her mind, sweeping her away, promising her the kind of delight she had always longed for and never yet experienced.

But, though his kisses were hungry and passionate, apparently holding himself in check, he made no move to take things further.

Knowing he was as aroused as she was, and bewildered by his restraint, her whole body crying out for more, she pressed herself against him.

As though he had been waiting for a signal, he ran a single finger up and down her spine. The caress was unexpected and thrilling, and she quivered like a violin being played.

Then while one hand cradled the back of her head, the other began to move over her, following the slender curve of waist and hip and buttock. At the same time his mouth left hers to stray down to the warm hollow at the base of her throat, where his tongue-tip proceeded to cause havoc.

She gave a little murmur of pleasure, convinced that there could be nothing more erotic—until he touched her breast, cupping the soft weight and brushing his thumb over the nipple, which instantly grew firm.

By the time he slid the straps of her dress off her shoulders to expose her small, beautifully shaped breasts, she was prey to the kind of sexual excitement she hadn't known existed.

When he bent his head and put his mouth to her breast the needle-sharp sensations his suckling caused were so exquisite that, unable at that moment to stand any more, she gave a little incoherent exclamation and made to push him away.

Straightening up at once, he adjusted the bodice of her dress with care, and eased the straps back into place, before saying coolly, 'I'm sorry if I'm not coming up to Jason's standard...'

Feeling like someone who had been enjoying a thrilling roller-coaster ride and was suddenly thrown off to land half-stunned and dazed, she just stared at him.

'I'd better say goodnight and let you get some sleep,' he added. 'We've a longish journey ahead of us tomorrow.'

He turned on his heel in the semi-darkness and walked away. A moment later his bedroom door closed quietly behind him.

It was clear that he had completely misunderstood her instinctive withdrawal. Shocked by the swift and totally unexpected ending to his lovemaking, she began to tremble violently.

He had talked about not coming up to Jason's standard, but he had far outstripped it.

Jason, always very self-orientated, wasn't in the same class for sensitivity and skill. Because he was always focused entirely on his own needs rather than on his partner's, interested only in reaching his objective rather than in the journey there, his lovemaking had been both cursory and clumsy.

It seemed dreadfully disloyal to even think such a thing, but it didn't make it any less true, and she found herself marvelling that she had never realised it before.

After a few kisses, if Jason decided he wasn't getting anywhere, regarding it as a waste of time, he would give up and sulk.

Whereas Gray had set out to give her pleasure, and had succeeded beyond her wildest dreams.

Her body still quivering with unappeased desire, her legs unsteady, her mind in a turmoil, she went through to her room and, switching on the light, sank down on the bed.

Where earlier in the evening she had felt dog-tired and only too eager to get some sleep, now she was wide awake and restless, frustration gnawing at her.

Perhaps a shower would help her to relax?

In desperation she seized on the stray thought, and, having stripped off her clothes, went through to the bathroom and cleaned her teeth before stepping into the glass cubicle.

She stood beneath the flow of hot water until her skin tingled, but it made no difference to how she felt inside.

When she had dried herself, rubbing the fine skin with unnecessary vigour, she took the pins from her hair and, her movements jerky, picked up her brush.

While she brushed out the thick, silky mass she tried to tell herself that it was just as well things had ended as they had. There was no way *she* could have called a halt, and if Gray hadn't backed off when he did it would have been too late.

She ought to be grateful.

But she wasn't.

Still aching with frustration and misery, she longed to be in his arms, yearned to have him satisfy the hunger he had so effortlessly aroused.

Fool! she berated herself angrily. How could she be thinking that way? No matter how skilful his lovemaking, all he wanted was a holiday fling, and she had never gone in for casual flings or affairs. It just wasn't in her nature.

Though as far as *she* was concerned, this wouldn't have been just a casual fling, soon over and easily forgotten. Something deep inside, something she couldn't put a name to, responded to Gray in a way she had never responded to anyone else.

Until now, she had regarded sex and love as going hand in hand, with love the more important of the two. But perhaps because of her childhood she had been afraid of strong feelings, wary of falling in love, knowing that love made one vulnerable.

Only Jason had come anywhere near to breaking through her defences. But in the end she had even held back with him, a man she had loved.

So where did that leave her? Was she going to remain a virgin all her life? Die without ever becoming a wife and mother? Or at the very least without knowing what it was like to be made love to by a man she wanted.

And she *did* want Gray Gallagher.

Pulling on a white towelling robe that hung behind the door, she returned to the bedroom as tense as when she had left it.

Her cotton nightdress lay limply across the double bed like the heroine of some Victorian melodrama. But *she* was no Victorian heroine. Perhaps by today's standards she was old-fashioned, with outmoded principles, but she was still a modern woman, able to choose her own path through life.

Gray was the only man who had ever made her long to throw her bonnet over the windmill. But from now on, having mistaken her reaction for rejection, she felt oddly certain that he would make no further move.

If she did want him as a lover, it was up to her to go to him and tell him so.

Giving herself no more time to think, barefoot, her hair tumbled in loose curls around her shoulders, she padded across the semi-dark living-room to his door.

She had raised her hand to knock when she realised she couldn't possibly do it. He might look at her with cool surprise.

That would be all it would take to make her want to curl up and die. She had none of the confidence of the truly liberated woman. In sexual matters she might follow, but she could never lead. Never take the initiative.

She was turning away when the door opened with a suddenness that made her give a startled gasp.

Gray stood in the doorway, his back to the light, wearing a short, navy-blue silk dressing gown.

'Something wrong?' he queried levelly.

'N-no... Yes...'

'Which?'

'I—I'd like to talk to you.'

'I was just about to fetch my laptop and catch up on some work.'

Boldly, she said, 'I couldn't sleep either.'

'Frustration's hell,' he agreed. 'Or are you going to tell me you're not frustrated?'

'If I told you that it wouldn't be true.' She looked at him pleadingly.

'Sorry, but on the earlier showing I wouldn't make a good stand-in for Jason, and I should hate to be found wanting.'

Gritting her teeth, she said, 'I don't want you to be a stand-in for Jason.'

'So what do you want?'

It was clear that he was going to give her no help. Swallowing, she said, 'I just want to make it clear that when I pushed you away it was because I... I...'

When he simply waited, she finished desperately, 'It was absolutely nothing to do with Jason.'

'You just couldn't stand me.'

'If I couldn't stand you, would I be here now? Wouldn't I be in my own bed, breathing a sigh of relief that I'd managed to escape your clutches?'

Though she couldn't see his face clearly, she was aware that he had relaxed.

'Well, it's nice to know that my sex appeal isn't quite on a par with Count Dracula's.'

'There's nothing wrong with your sex appeal, it's…' She hesitated.

'Appealing?' he suggested, tongue-in-cheek.

Unwilling to be laughed at in such trying circumstances, she retorted, 'At any rate it's better than your comprehension. You totally misinterpreted my reaction.'

'It seemed pretty clear at the time. You didn't exactly clutch me to your bosom.'

Her face burning with heat, she said crossly, 'Have you never heard of sensual overload?'

'Are you trying to tell me it was sensual overload that caused your reaction?'

'I'm not *trying* to tell you. I *am* telling you.'

'I see. Does it happen often?'

'It's never happened to me before,' she said, and immediately regretted her honesty.

'Well, well, well…' he murmured derisively, 'and here I was, jealous of Jason.'

Hating his mockery, she burst out, 'If you think it was easy for me to come…' Then, suddenly close to tears, she stopped speaking abruptly and turned away.

He caught her wrist. 'Don't rush off.'

She tried to jerk free. 'I'm not staying here to be made fun of.'

'My little love, I'm not making fun of you.'

Flustered by the casual endearment, she stopped trying to pull away, and, using the wrist he was still holding, he drew her unresisting into the bedroom and closed the door behind them.

CHAPTER SIX

'I *WASN'T* making fun of you,' he repeated. 'If anything I was mocking myself.'

'Why should you be doing that?'

'For taking myself far too seriously. However, I'll do my best to make it up to you.'

He waited, one eyebrow raised expectantly.

When she said nothing, he suggested, 'Aren't you going to ask me how?'

Warily, convinced he was teasing her, she went along with it. 'All right, how?'

'I thought I might teach you how to cope with sensual overload.'

Finding herself suddenly breathless, she asked, 'How would you do that?'

His eyes gleaming, he answered, 'By giving you plenty of practice.'

She began to tremble.

'But we'll take it slowly, shall we?'

He slid his hands into the wide sleeves of her robe to hold her elbows and draw her to him. When their faces were only inches apart, he stopped and smiled down at her.

Their bodies weren't touching, but she was very aware of how close they were and the warmth of his hands cupping her elbows.

Lifting her face to his, like a flower to the sun, she was waiting for his kiss when he surprised her by suggesting softly, 'Why don't *you* kiss *me*?'

Her eyes flying to his mouth, a mouth that sent shivers up and down her spine, she hesitated for an instant, *wanting* to kiss him, but oddly shy. Then, gathering her courage, she stood on tiptoe and touched her lips to his.

For a moment he remained quite still, making no effort to kiss her back, and, disconcerted, she was about to draw away when his lips moved in response, returning the slight pressure.

At first his kiss was chaste, but soon it changed to teasing and sensual as his mouth coaxed hers to part and he ran the tip of his tongue delicately along the silky inner skin of her upper lip.

While his kisses became ever more tantalising and erotic, he withdrew his hands from her sleeves and, unfastening her robe, slipped it off her shoulders and lifted her onto the bed.

Lying in a pool of golden light cast by the bedside lamp, she gazed up at him, her whole body waiting, anticipating, responsive to a trustworthy lover.

He sat down beside her and his hands began to travel lightly over her, stroking and caressing as they went, seeking out every erogenous zone.

Feeling the shudders that ran through her, he drew back a little and asked, 'Going too fast for you?'

'No.'

'That's my girl.'

While one hand lingered on her breast to tease a pink nipple between finger and thumb, the other moved down to her stomach. When his exploring fingers found the warm, satiny skin of her inner thighs and the nest of silky brown curls, she couldn't repress a gasp.

'Get ready for it,' he warned softly, and, nuzzling his face against her breast, laved the other erect nipple before taking it into his mouth.

Everything she had so far experienced paled into insignificance, and, turning her head from side to side on the pillow, she began to make little mewling sounds deep in her throat.

The exquisite sensations he was creating were growing, tightening, escalating, until her entire being was concentrated on the release of that spiralling pleasure.

When it happened, her eyes closed, her whole body rigid now, helpless in the grip of such intense delight, she cried out.

For a while she lay quivering, before becoming quiet and still, utterly relaxed, lapped in a bliss as sensual and satisfying as warm, scented bath water.

She felt a gentle kiss on the tip of her nose, and opened her eyes to find Gray looking down at her, his expression oddly tender.

'Thank you,' she said simply.

'Has anyone told you you're an absolute delight to make love to?'

She shook her head.

'Not even Jason?'

Jason had never touched her so intimately.

When, haltingly, she said so, Gray looked staggered. 'I know you were holding back from total commitment, but surely you must have done some heavy petting occasionally? Just to keep him interested. To remind him what he was missing.'

'No, we didn't.'

'You mean your relationship went no further than a few kisses?'

'Yes.' Her voice wry, she added, 'Considering he's now my brother-in-law, it's just as well.'

A look of relief on his face, Gray murmured, 'Well, I'll be damned! Unless he was getting his kicks elsewhere, he must have been hellish frustrated.'

A thought struck her, and she asked a shade anxiously, 'What about you?'

Instantly on her wavelength, he smiled. 'I didn't miss out. Your body's so responsive I believe I enjoyed it even more than you did.'

A little embarrassed now, she was wondering why he'd chosen that way to pleasure her, when he added, 'And it served to release a little of your tension. Now we can take things slowly, make our lovemaking even more enjoyable, so that you'll never want the night to end.'

She found it hard to believe that anything could be *more* enjoyable. In any case, as far as she was concerned her previous hunger had been well and truly appeased. She was sated.

Watching her expressive face, he grinned. 'Don't you believe it. That was merely the hors d'oeuvre.'

He rose to his feet and, untying the belt, stripped off his dressing gown.

Watching him, she caught her breath and her throat went dry. Oh, but he was beautiful…virile…magnificent… Adjectives rushed into her mind, but none of them did him justice.

He was every woman's dream lover.

Narrow-hipped and broad across the shoulders, his whole body as well-proportioned as any Greek statue, he carried not an ounce of spare flesh, and in the lamplight his smooth skin gleamed like oiled silk.

Slipping in beside her, he added, 'But before we start the feast, I suggest we experiment a little first to see what you enjoy the most.'

'I really don't think…' she began. Then stopped abruptly as, with just the slightest pressure of a single finger, he brought the desire she had thought dead back to glorious life.

When she awoke and opened her eyes, daylight was filling the room. A glance at her watch told her it was late morning. She was alone in the big bed, but she could hear the shower running.

Remembering the previous night, she wondered what on earth had got into her. She could scarcely believe she had acted so completely out of character, abandoning herself so wantonly and passionately to a man she had only just met. A man she knew virtually nothing about.

Yet she had. And though it went against all her principles to indulge in a short holiday affair, she found that for perhaps the first time in her adult life she felt like a real woman, glowingly alive and supremely confident.

There was no way she could regret what had happened. It had been utter bliss. Gray had proved to be a fantastic lover. Generous and sensitive, he had known exactly what to do with his body and hers.

She had heard lovemaking described as skyrockets and fireworks; a soaring flight to the stars; stepping out of a plane at ten thousand feet; and, most poetic of all, a little death.

It had been all of those and more. A lifetime's experience crammed into one night.

Freshly awakened, and new to such pleasures, her body had welcomed his without restraint. In return he had been gentle and considerate, careful not to leave her bruised or tender.

Afterwards, as she lay contentedly in his arms, he had said, 'So I really am the first!'

Feeling her face grow warm, she'd answered, 'I'm afraid so. Do you mind?'

'Far from it. However, I must admit to being surprised. Though you tried to make it clear you were a nice, old-fashioned girl, I wasn't sure such a thing existed these days.'

'If I really *were* a nice, old-fashioned girl I wouldn't be in your bed now.'

'But when you accepted my offer of a holiday, you didn't intend this to happen, did you?'

'No.'

'So why *are* you in my bed? No, don't bother to answer that question. I know why, of course.'

Looking up at him through long curly lashes, she teased, 'You consider yourself irresistible?'

'Hardly.'

'Then why *do* you think I'm here?'

'A backlash from Jason,' he said. 'After losing out on that score—'

'This has absolutely nothing to do with Jason,' she denied hardly.

Gray was unconvinced. 'Surely it must have. After years of celibacy, why let your hair down now?'

'Perhaps I'd grown tired of being a virgin.'

'You mean when you found you couldn't swop that virginity for a wedding ring you decided to have some fun instead?'

'No, that's not what I mean.'

'Then why *me*?'

'I found you...attractive.'

'You're twenty-three. You must have found plenty of other men attractive.'

'Very few. I suppose I'm just hard to please.'

'Well, I hope you're not disappointed. You've ended up with a holiday instead of a honeymoon and a lover instead of a bridegroom. It must seem a poor consolation prize.'

Somehow the thought of what she had lost no longer had the power to hurt, and, refusing to be rattled, she said lightly, 'As consolation prizes go, I think it's a pretty good one.'

She felt him relax, and the hand that had been lying on her ribcage moved up to caress her breast. 'For that, you deserve a reward.'

A little smile hovering on her lips, she was reliving that 'reward' when the bathroom door opened and Gray appeared, wearing a short robe, a towel slung round his neck.

Newly shaved, his black hair plastered seal-like to his well-shaped head and his green eyes gleaming between thick, sooty lashes, he looked so appealing and virile that her heart turned over.

'Good morning,' he greeted her cheerfully, and, crossing to the bed, dropped a light kiss on her lips.

He smelt of shower gel and aftershave, and tasted of minty toothpaste. She found that healthy freshness a powerful aphrodisiac.

Lifting the towel to vigorously rub his hair, he told her, 'Breakfast, or, rather, brunch, should be here in a minute or so. Would you like it in bed?'

Feeling unwashed and tangly-haired, and needing to clean her teeth, she pushed herself into a sitting position and hastily refused. 'No, I'd like a shower first, so I'll get up. How much time have we got?'

Discarding the towel, he said, 'Plenty. We don't need to leave for the airport until early afternoon.' His eyes were on her breasts and, as though he'd touched them, her nipples grew firm under his appreciative gaze.

Trying desperately to appear casual, she pulled up the duvet to cover her nakedness, and looked around for her robe. It was well out of reach.

In spite of, or perhaps *because* of all that had happened the previous night, she felt suddenly shy, reluctant to get out of bed in front of him.

'Please could you pass my robe?'

Straight-faced, he said, 'Of course. Though it's so warm I doubt if you'll need it.'

He reached for the robe, but instead of handing it to her he held it ready, leaving her no alternative but to push back the duvet and climb out.

Knowing she was blushing, Rebecca was glad he couldn't see her face as she slid into it.

Folding his arms round her, he drew her back against him and, proving he missed very little, leaned forward to blow on her hot cheek, making her blush even harder.

Then, sounding remorseful, 'My love, it's a shame to tease you.'

'If you really think that, why do you keep doing it?' she demanded.

'You look so enchanting when you blush, I can't resist it.'

'Try.'

His cheek against hers, his crossed hands busy inside her robe, he suggested, 'If you want any help with that shower...?'

Her breath coming quickly, and afraid that at any moment she might weaken, she said repressively, 'No, thank you,' and, pulling herself free, fled, followed by his soft laughter.

Used to having a slice of morning toast and a cup of coffee, standing alone in her small kitchen, it was strange and exciting to be sitting opposite Gray while they drank fresh orange juice and tucked into crisp curls of bacon, maple syrup and pancakes.

His disturbing sexuality leashed, he was a pleasant companion, quietly good-humoured, happy to talk or simply eat in companionable silence.

Dressed in well-cut cords and a casual shirt, he still contrived to look like a man of authority.

Her eyes lingering on his lean, suntanned face with its fine, straight nose and those extraordinary eyes beneath level black brows, she wondered how she could ever have thought him less handsome than Jason.

He had a bone structure that would keep him looking good even when he was old, whereas Jason had the kind of matinée-idol looks that by middle-age would start to grow slack and pouchy.

When the feeling of betrayal that should have followed this disloyal thought failed to arrive, she was surprised.

'You're looking very serious,' Gray remarked, reaching to pour her coffee. 'What's on your mind?'

'I was thinking about Jason.'

His face darkening with a sudden anger, Gray burst out, 'Damn the man!' Then more quietly, 'Love's the very devil…'

But did she still love Jason?

Even as her mind started to frame the question, she knew she didn't.

The spell he had undoubtedly cast had faded and died, and so had her love. Otherwise she could never have given herself so completely to another man.

'But if you can put your feelings for Jason aside, I hope you'll find that coming with me is preferable to sitting at home alone.'

She was about to tell him that she no longer had any feelings for Jason, when he went on, 'Neither of us want any new emotional entanglements. Which means we'll be free to simply enjoy ourselves with no danger of getting involved or asking more than the other person is willing to give.

'It could work pretty well. Wouldn't you agree?'

It was only common sense, but somehow it sounded so cold-blooded that she felt chilled.

As she hesitated he asked sharply, 'You're not having second thoughts about last night?'

'No,' she answered, her golden eyes meeting his.

His faint sigh of relief was audible, before he pursued, 'About the holiday?'

'No.'

'That's good.' He smiled his slow smile at her.

She thought wonderingly that it was less than forty-eight hours since they had met, but in some strange way it was as if she had always known him, as if he'd become part of her life, necessary to her.

No, she mustn't let herself think that way. He was her first, and would probably be her only lover, so he would always be very special to her. But she couldn't let him become *necessary*.

After this holiday they would be going their separate ways and he would probably never give her another thought.

All she had was the coming two weeks, so instead of repining she would enjoy every moment of them to the full and then, grateful for what fate had bestowed on her, let go…

They were in a taxi on their way to the airport, when Gray's mobile rang.

Having excused himself, he lifted the phone to his ear and spoke crisply. 'Gallagher… Yes… Yes… Excellent… Even better… Yes, we're quite prepared to match that… Yes, straight away… Thanks for letting me know…' With a glance at Rebecca, he added, 'I will, certainly.'

Dropping the small instrument back into his pocket, he told her calmly, 'That was Scrivener.'

'Has he come to a decision?' she asked eagerly.

'Yes. He's carrying on, as I thought he would.'

As she breathed a sigh of relief, Gray continued, 'The really good news is that, instead of putting a limit on further injections of cash, he's going all out. The sky's the limit. Whatever it takes to really get the complex up and running.'

'Oh, that's great!'

'It's better than I'd dared hope,' he admitted. 'And it's all due to you.'

When she began to demur, he shook his head. 'We both know it's the truth. Scrivener said so too.'

With a slight frown, as if the idea displeased him, Gray added, 'He also said that if you were looking for a new post and had no objection to working in Boston, he would be delighted to offer you a job as his PA.'

Surprise kept her silent for a moment, then she demurred, 'But Jason told me he always has a male secretary and PA.'

'That was because his last wife didn't trust him. In

the end, apparently tired of her endless jealousy, he divorced her.

'But in spite of three previous marriages he's still childless, so, needing a son and heir, he's apparently looking around for wife number four.'

'Marianne?' she suggested.

'I very much doubt it. Scrivener's no fool. Marianne and the others like her fulfil a need, but they're not wife material. When it comes to marriage he always chooses a woman with brains and character, as well as beauty.

'*You* seem to have made a distinct hit with our Andrew, so if you *were* looking for a wealthy husband it's my opinion you'd be in there with a chance.'

Rebecca shuddered inwardly. There was no way she would want to marry a man like Scrivener.

But Gray was going on, 'You could do a lot worse. Apparently where his women are concerned he's quite generous. It could be a marvellous opportunity for any woman who was willing to close her eyes to his extramarital activities, and simply enjoy the kind of lifestyle he can offer.'

His cynical words hurt.

Unwilling, however, to show it, she remarked lightly, 'I'll bear that in mind,' and saw by his expression that for some reason her answer had ruffled him.

Perhaps, still not fully convinced that she *hadn't* been after Jason's money, he'd been testing her?

Gray, for his part, was wishing he'd never brought up the subject of Scrivener remarrying. He'd been expecting Rebecca to protest vehemently that she *wasn't* looking for a wealthy husband, and could *never* bring herself to marry anyone like Scrivener. Instead she appeared to be considering the possibility.

He tried to tell himself that it didn't matter a jot if she *was*.

But somehow it did.

Scowling, he wondered if she would contact Scrivener

about the job offer, and take it from there. If she did, he only had himself to blame for putting the idea into her head.

Unhappy with the situation, Rebecca was about to try and retrieve it when, noticing that scowl, she chickened out, and the journey to Logan Airport was completed in a not altogether comfortable silence.

Gray's black mood persisted until they had boarded the small plane and were taxiing down the runway ready for take-off.

Then, having thought it through a dozen times, and coming to believe he had almost certainly misjudged her reaction, he turned to Rebecca and, giving her a smile, took her hand.

Catching her surprised expression, he said, 'You don't look scared this time, but it's a good excuse to hold your hand and apologise for my bad temper.'

Her happiness restored, she smiled back.

'Does that smile mean I'm forgiven?'

'It would if there was anything to forgive.'

'Generous woman.'

He lowered their clasped hands, and his knuckles grazed her thigh, making her jump. 'If you're in agreement, I thought that in a while we might resume our game.'

His eyes on her face, he waited, a slight smile tugging at his lips.

After a moment she recalled how, on the plane, he'd brought her tea in bed and deliberately sat too close. Then his comment, 'I've found it most entertaining, and I look forward to resuming later.'

Demurely, she said, 'Oh, *that* game. Well, perhaps this time, before we start, we should lay down some ground rules?'

He raised a dark, level brow. 'What had you in mind? Clothes on and hands off?'

Boldly, she asked, 'Where's the fun in that?'

'Well, provided you promise not to seduce me...'

She pretended to think about it. 'OK, I'll go along with that, so long as I don't have to stop you if you try to seduce me.'

'That's my girl.'

'After all,' she added seriously, 'it might be my only chance to join the Mile-High Club.'

Then, finding the idea gave her no pleasure, 'I presume you're a fully fledged member by now?'

'As a matter of fact I haven't yet joined.'

Though it shouldn't have made any difference, it did, and his answer brought a swift rush of mingled relief and gladness.

It had been cool and grey when they left Boston, but they landed at San Francisco International Airport in dazzling sunshine and, on Rebecca's part at least, a cloud of euphoria.

Because of the time difference it was still afternoon, and the Californian sun beat down fiercely. As soon as they left the air-conditioned terminal building, the heat struck through the thin soles of her sandals and seemed to envelope her in a sticky embrace.

She was pleased she'd decided on a sleeveless cotton dress, and taken her ash-brown hair up into a smooth coil.

A sleek white car, its hood down, was waiting for them, and as soon as the driver had handed over the keys they set off north for what Gray told her was a longish drive to the Napa Valley.

Though the air was hot and sticky with humidity, the open-topped car was pleasantly cool as they joined the endless flow of traffic on the freeway.

Rebecca's first impression of the west coast was of continuous traffic, a straggle of unprepossessing glass and concrete skyscrapers, and towering advertisement hoardings lining the roadside.

All the same, with so much to look back on and so much to look forward to, she felt as excited as a child on Christmas morning.

After a while Gray raised his voice above the wind and the engine noise and the soft phut of insects hitting the windscreen, to enquire, 'Do you want to press on, or stop for a bite to eat *en route*?'

Not at all hungry, and finding the smell of gasoline and onions from the roadside pull-ins distinctly unappealing, she said, 'Press on, if it's all the same to you.'

His look of relief seemed to suggest that he shared her feelings. But then, she was starting to discover, they were more often than not in tune.

While she enjoyed the sun on her face and listened to the soothing shush of the tyres, her mind went back to earlier that afternoon.

Recalling Gray's skilful lovemaking, she shivered deliciously, the mere remembrance making her heart race until it was difficult to breathe.

Saying, 'If we're going to join the club we might as well do it in style,' he had made love to her time and time again, with a kind of sweet ruthlessness that had left her quivering with pleasure, and emotionally exhausted.

She would have slept, but the hours had flown by and there had been no time for sleep...

Glancing sideways at her, Gray saw that, though her eyes were closed, a little smile still played around her lips.

Resisting a sudden mad urge to stop the car and kiss those smiling lips, he admitted to himself that he couldn't get enough of this woman.

She was like no one else he had ever met.

He had discovered that she was vulnerable in some ways, tough in others, shy and uncertain, yet remarkably self-controlled.

At first, in spite of her declared love for Jason, she had struck him as cool, sexually. Now he knew that coolness was only on the surface. A façade to hide behind. Underneath she was fiery and passionate, as hot-blooded as he himself.

He was well aware that Jason, though weak in many ways, was a charming and ruthless predator with a powerful sex appeal. How in heaven's name had a passionate woman, who was also in love with him, managed to hold out against his blandishments?

It was a question Gray couldn't really answer, but he found himself absurdly pleased that she *had*. She was too good for Jason.

Even if he had been on the level about marrying her— and in view of his past record that was unlikely—within weeks he would have been unfaithful, and she would have found herself saddled with a husband she could neither trust nor respect.

During the drive, while Gray was busy with his thoughts, Rebecca dozed intermittently, half waking from time to time, before drifting off again.

When she awoke fully and opened her eyes, they were in what she guessed was the Napa Valley. Sitting up straighter, she looked around her.

On either side the ground was rolling and fertile, its brilliant green just beginning to take on a slightly parched look that suggested a long spell of dry weather.

Slanting her a glance, Gray said, 'The road we're on now is the St Helena Highway, known as the vineyard road.'

'Have we far to go?'

'It shouldn't be too far. According to the directions I was given, the Santa Rosa spread is about fourteen or fifteen miles from Napa itself, and we drove through the town just a few minutes ago.'

After a while they skirted a small outcrop of hills and the wide, flat valley began to close in. Soon there were steepish slopes on either side, and they were in the vineyards.

'This should be our turning,' Gray said, and took a narrow road to the left.

At the bottom of the road a pair of tall iron gates were standing open. Across an archway above them, black wrought-iron letters bore the legend 'Santa Rosa Wineries'.

They drove through the gates and up a long drive, finally stopping in front of a white, one-storey, Spanish-style hacienda. Its tiled veranda had a series of archways and was festooned with climbing plants and bright with tubs of flowers.

A small, battered pick-up truck was parked close by. As they climbed out of the car, a woman appeared in the nearest archway dressed in red cotton trousers and a loose yellow top. A red and yellow spotted bandanna was tied around her head, and her bare feet were pushed into a pair of ancient sneakers.

'You must be Mr Gallagher.' Coming down the steps, she thrust out a thin brown hand.

'That's right.' Having shaken her hand, Gray drew Rebecca forward. 'And this is Miss Ferris.'

Again the hand shot out. 'Hi! I'm Gloria Redford. Ben and I have been taking care of the place since Manuel's daughter helped him move out.

'Stubborn old fool,' she added fondly. 'Instead of trying to manage, he should have sold Santa Rosa and gone to live with his daughter five years ago when his son died.

'Well, now you're here, I'd best be getting back.'

'Have you far to go?' Rebecca asked politely.

'I live in Yountville, so it's not far, but Ben and the others will be wanting their supper.'

Turning to Gray, she added, 'Oh, and speaking of supper, there's a trolley in the larder laid all ready for you, and you'll find enough food in the fridge to last for the time being.

'I'll pop back in a day or so to see if there's any items I've missed. If you need anything in the meantime, or you want me to pop in to change the beds or tidy the place, just give me a ring. My number's on the board in the kitchen.'

'Thanks.'

With a cheery grin, she bounded off to the pick-up. The engine roared into life, and a second or two later she was driving away, a cloud of dust billowing after her.

While Gray retrieved their luggage from the boot, Rebecca stood staring at the house that was to be their holiday home for the next two weeks, and thought that never in the whole of her life had she felt so blissfully happy.

CHAPTER SEVEN

GLANCING at Rebecca, and struck by the glow on her face, Gray commented, 'You're looking very happy.'

'I *am* happy,' she said simply.

'Then let's hope we can keep it that way. Ready to take a look at the house?'

'You bet!'

She followed him up the veranda steps and through the door Gloria Redford had left open.

Putting their cases down, Gray suggested, 'Let's explore, shall we?'

The main living area ran from the front of the house through to the back. It was cool and spacious, with white walls, terrazzo flooring, lots of plants and the minimum of furniture.

There was a huge open fireplace of unplastered stone, and, to either side of the flower-filled hearth, tier upon tier of built-in bookcases, all of which were empty.

After a moment or two, Rebecca realised that it was the complete absence of any personal things that made it seem like the ideal summer layout for the cover of a glossy magazine.

At the far end, sliding glass panels led out to a paved patio. There was a brick-built barbecue and several comfortable-looking chairs and loungers grouped around a table. Beyond the patio was a swimming pool, the late-evening sun sparkling on its blue water.

On one side of the living area was a sizable kitchen with a cool larder, and beyond that two bedrooms and a bathroom.

At the opposite end of the house, two large, airy, *en suite* bedrooms led into each other. They seemed to be guest rooms, and identical apart from the fact that in one the duvet and rugs were thundercloud-blue, and in the other mulberry.

Both had a double bed, and were lined on one wall with white tongue-and-groove wardrobes. Light muslin curtains screened the long windows.

'As you're the guest,' Gray said, 'you get first choice. Which room would you like?'

Taken aback, because she had presumed he would want them to share, she stammered, 'I—I don't really mind. You choose.'

He grinned. 'I'd prefer whichever one *you're* in. But, having promised you a room of your own...'

She took a deep breath and asked, 'What if I said I didn't want a room of my own?'

'I was rather hoping you *would* say that.' He waited expectantly, one eyebrow cocked.

'I don't want a room of my own,' she obliged.

He dropped a quick kiss on her lips. 'Then let's share this one. It has a bathroom on either side, so at least you can have a bathroom of your own.'

With a fast-beating heart she went into the mulberry room, while Gray fetched their cases. Putting them on the bed, he queried, 'Shall we be exemplary and unpack straight away?'

If she were his wife, she would do it for him.

'Then, as soon as I've freshened up, I'll find the ingredients for a long, cold drink.'

'Sounds good.' Her voice was husky.

While she emptied her case and put away her things, Gray unpacked with a speed and efficiency that spoke of long practice in looking after himself.

Watching him covertly, she wondered why he had never married. It seemed strange that a man of his age, a man who appeared to have everything, hadn't been snapped up long since.

Unless he was one of those males who hated the thought of being tied down, and wanted the freedom to love all and marry none?

Busy with her thoughts, she unconsciously slowed down, and he easily finished first.

His case stowed neatly in the bottom of one of the cupboards, he picked up a change of clothing and disappeared into the nearest bathroom.

A moment or two later she heard the shower running.

Feeling hot and sticky, she decided to follow suit. Taking fresh undies and a skimpy button-through dress—bought especially for the Caribbean—she went into the second bathroom.

When she had showered and changed she brushed out her long hair and pulled it back into a loose knot, then, cool and refreshed, went in search of Gray.

She found him lounging on the patio, a tray of drinks at his elbow.

He rose to his feet at her approach and smiled at her. Wearing light trousers and an olive-green shirt open at the neck to expose the tanned column of his throat, he looked devastatingly attractive, and her heart turned over.

'What's it to be?' he asked.

'Fruit juice, please.'

Pulling forward a cushioned chair, he settled her into it, before lifting a glass jug and pouring two tall tumblers of juice chinking with ice.

'Thank you.' Accepting the tumbler he handed her, she leaned back and sipped appreciatively.

It was a lovely evening; the air was warm and as clear as glass, fragrant with the scent of flowering shrubs and full of the shrill sound of cicadas.

The sun had gone and a blue dusk was stealthily creeping in. Through the screen of vegetation, she could see lights beginning to twinkle on the opposite slope and along the valley floor.

Somewhere in the distance a dog barked, and closer at hand she could hear the faint sound of music and smell burning charcoal, as if the neighbours were having a barbecue.

When their drinks were finished, he rose to his feet and held out his hand. 'Shall we stretch our legs before we eat?'

She put her hand in his and, as always when he touched her, felt her skin tingle in response.

Fingers entwined, they made their way past the swimming pool, and descended a short flight of stone steps into a nicely kept garden.

As they strolled along the winding paths Rebecca watched a pale moon rise and hang low on the horizon, while the clear blue colour over the hills changed to a velvety purple and the stars above them grew bigger and brighter.

Unconsciously, she sighed.

'Why the sigh?' he asked.

'I was just thinking how beautiful it all is.'

'Then you're not sorry you decided to come?'

'Surprised, but not sorry,' she answered.

'Surprised?'

'It just wasn't like me. I mean…it's so completely out of character.'

He squeezed her hand. 'Well, I'm very glad you managed to step out of character for once.'

'Tell me something. If I'd refused to come, would you have carried out your threat to tell Philip Lorne what had happened between Jason and me?'

'What do you think?'

'I've no idea,' she admitted. 'I know so little about you.'

'Yet you trusted me.'

'I suppose I must have done.'

'Do you still?'

'Yes.'

'In spite of the fact that we're now lovers?'

'It was as much my doing as yours.'

'And you don't regret it?'

'No.'

'What if I told you I have a live-in lover stashed away at home?'

Just for an instant shock scattered her wits, then, collecting herself, she asked evenly, 'Have you?'

'No. A couple of months ago my live-in lover left me for someone else.'

'How long had you been together?'

'Just over a year.'

Though his face gave no clue as to how upset he was, she said, 'I'm sorry.'

'There's no need to be. Any feeling I had for her died a long time ago.

'Though Cleo is one of the most beautiful women I've ever set eyes on, I soon discovered that her nature didn't match.

'Our sleeping together gradually became just a matter of habit and convenience, and, as she was hardly ever at home when I was, companionship ceased to exist. We might have drifted on for a while longer if she hadn't met a retired oilman with more millions than he could spend. Tex, she assured me, was prepared to give her everything she wanted, and quite happy to indulge her every whim.

'I wished her luck.'

As they rounded the corner of the house and found themselves back on the patio, Rebecca said, 'Even so, it's bound to be sad, breaking up with someone you once loved.'

Seeing the glow had gone from her face, and cursing himself for a fool, he changed the subject. 'Now, where would you like to eat? Inside or out?'

'Outside, if that suits you? It's much too nice to be indoors.'

Nodding his approval, he suggested, 'Then pull up a lounger while I go and fetch our supper.'

He was back quite quickly, wheeling a trolley covered with butter muslin. A white linen napkin was draped over his arm.

She was surprised to see that his hair was parted in the middle and slicked down smoothly with water.

He whipped off the muslin to display a simple meal of ham, soft cheese, green salad and fat, rosy peaches. Then, shoulders rounded, head bobbing, he said unctuously, 'At your service, madam. What can I help you to?'

She could never have imagined him playing the fool, and, struggling to keep a straight face, she said, 'Thank you, James. I'd like some cheese and salad.' He filled a plate, then looked up to ask, 'And will madam have a glass of wine? I understand it's the produce of Santa Rosa.'

His crossed eyes were her undoing, and she burst out laughing. When she could control her mirth sufficiently, she warned, 'If the wind changes, you'll stay like that.'

He came to lean over her, leering. 'If I do, will you still like me?'

'Oh, certainly,' she said and lifted her hand to ruffle his damp hair, while helpless laughter bubbled up inside her.

'You're not taking this seriously,' he complained, and stopped her laughter with a series of kisses.

Kisses that went on and on, growing more fervent, blowing her mind, while he dealt with the buttons of her dress.

He was easing down her dainty briefs when, snatching at the coat tails of sanity, she gasped, 'Don't! Someone might come.'

Grinning down at her, he whispered in her ear, 'Both of us, I hope.'

Then with a quick movement he flattened the lounger completely, and followed her down.

*   *   *

It was some time before they got round to thinking about food, and when they did Gray opened the bottle of Santa Rosa Chenin Blanc.

When they had both tried the wine, he asked, 'What's your opinion?'

'I'm no expert,' Rebecca said.

'Nor are ninety per cent of the people who drink wine. Just tell me what you think of it.'

'I like it. It's nice and fresh and fruity.'

He switched on the patio lights, and, having held up his glass to judge the colour and clearness of the wine, he took another thoughtful sip.

'Mmm... If we decide to produce ordinary table wine for a year or two while we do some replanting, this could be a reasonable proposition.'

'Then the vineyard's still in production?'

'After a fashion. Though the vines have been taken care of and the grapes continually harvested, for several years now no wine has actually been produced on the premises.

'One of the big neighbouring concerns, who make and bottle huge volumes of both red and white table wine, have bought Santa Rosa's grapes to blend with their own.

'They'll probably do the same this year. But once we're up and running it will be different.'

'Will you be in competition?'

He shook his head. 'Rather than simply producing drinkable table wine, I'd prefer to concentrate on the production of fine wines. It's more challenging, and, if successful, extremely lucrative.'

'How soon could you start?'

'That would depend on the established grape varieties, and on what kind of plant there is. Tomorrow we can take a look at the winery building, if you're at all interested?'

'Oh, yes, I am,' she said eagerly. 'It sounds absolutely fascinating.'

Stretched side by side on loungers, they talked for a while

about wine and the vineyard's prospects, then gradually fell silent.

It was very late, but, euphoric and enjoying the magic of the night, they continued to sit there.

After a while Gray reached out and, taking her hand, held it, his thumb gently massaging her palm.

She shivered.

It was so romantic that she thought with a strange kind of longing, *this could be our honeymoon...*

Only of course it wasn't.

As far as she and Gray were concerned this was a mere holiday fling, a short-term affair with no commitment on either side.

It was Lisa and Jason who were on honeymoon, enjoying a romantic start to their new life together as man and wife.

Sighing, she wondered, what if the fairy godmother she had believed in as a child could wave a magic wand and give her the chance to swop places with Lisa? Would she take it?

No, she wouldn't.

Looking back, she could see that she had been falling out of love with Jason for a long time without realising it.

Freed from that emotional burden, she could now accept that he belonged in the past, and rejoice because his defection was no longer an ever-present regret lying like a dark shadow on her mind...

As though her thoughts had disturbed him, Gray turned his head to glance at her. 'You look very pensive,' he remarked.

'I was thinking about—' Suddenly recalling his angry reaction last time she had mentioned Jason, she stopped speaking abruptly, a spot of colour creeping into her cheeks.

His jaw tightened. 'Jason, presumably?'

Seeing by her expression that he'd hit the nail on the head, his voice curt, he said, 'You seem to do little else.

Did you think about him when we were in bed? Imagine it was him making love to you rather than me?'

'N-no, of course not,' she stammered. 'As a matter of fact, I...'

About to tell him that she no longer loved Jason, she hesitated. If she did, would he think she'd just been pretending all along? That she really *had* just been after Jason's money?

He obviously didn't totally trust her on that score, otherwise he wouldn't have taunted her about Andrew Scrivener.

And surely it couldn't matter to him what her feelings for Jason were? *He* had no interest in her, apart from a sexual one.

Hadn't he laid it on the line? 'Neither of us want any new emotional entanglements...'

She took a deep, steadying breath, and went on, 'As a matter of fact I was just thinking about Lisa and Jason enjoying their honeymoon.'

'You visualise a romantic one, no doubt?' Gray enquired sarcastically.

Refusing to be put down, she said quietly, 'I think honeymoons *should* be romantic.'

'Presumably you've never been on one.'

'No.' Almost to herself, she added, 'And I probably never will.'

'I'm sorry,' Gray said, his fingers tightening around hers. 'I'm being a brute to you. But I'm not in the mood for such sentimental claptrap.'

'You're a cynic,' she accused.

'Better a cynic than a romantic.'

'You really *do* hate the idea of romance.'

'I think of it as the old Chinese curse.'

'What Chinese curse?'

'May all your dreams come true.'

'Oh...'

'Believe me, honeymoons aren't necessarily either romantic or happy, and it's my guess that Lisa and Jason are unlikely to be enjoying theirs.'

Withdrawing her hand, Rebecca sat up straighter. 'What makes you say that?'

'All the signs indicate that it will very quickly develop into a battleground, so if you're thinking *happy ever after*, forget it.'

Shocked, she cried, 'I don't know how you can say such a thing!'

'Because it's the truth,' he said wearily.

'I don't believe it.'

'Think,' he urged her seriously. 'What kind of woman is Lisa?'

Without waiting for an answer, he went on, 'Beautiful undoubtedly, charming when she wants to be, but shallow and spoilt, selfish to the core, wilful, scheming and deceitful, wouldn't you say?'

Rebecca flinched. 'She may be all of those, but she's a lot of other things as well. She can be caring and thoughtful—'

But Gray was going on relentlessly, 'And what kind of man is Jason?'

Again he answered his own question. 'Handsome undoubtedly, charming when it suits him, but just as shallow and spoilt, as selfish and wilful, as scheming and deceitful as his new wife.

'Can you really see any hope for them...?'

Battered by words as though they were stones, she just wanted to crawl away.

'*I* can't,' Gray added. 'Especially when he discovers how she's lied to him.'

'Lied to him?'

'Then she didn't tell you?'

'Tell me what?'

'That she was pregnant.'

Rebecca's jaw dropped.

'No, I can see she didn't.' Gray's voice was grim.

'I don't believe it,' she said flatly.

Her stepsister had once confided that she had no intention of ever having children. That she had taken, and would always take, every precaution to make sure she never became pregnant.

'You must be mistaken,' she insisted. 'Lisa doesn't like babies. She would have taken care.'

Gray smiled grimly. 'I don't doubt it.'

Pulling herself together with an effort, she demanded, 'Then what makes you think she's pregnant?'

'Jason thinks so.'

'How do you know?'

'Let's say I heard it on the grapevine. I guess he must have confided in someone that that was why the wedding was taking place in such a hurry.

'I feel sure he was right, as far as it goes. But not for the obvious reason, that the blushing bride didn't want to appear pregnant.'

She frowned. 'What other reason could there be?'

'That your dear stepsister didn't want to chance being found out, and every month that passed increased the risk.'

'I don't know what you're getting at.'

As though speaking to a not-very-bright child, he explained, 'I don't believe for a moment that she's pregnant, and as she and Jason were living together he was bound to discover the truth sooner or later.'

'But why should she tell him she was pregnant if she wasn't?'

'It's one of the oldest tricks in the book. I'm only surprised Jason fell for it.'

Rebecca shook her head as if to clear it. 'I can't see why she would need to lie, when they were going to be married anyway.'

'I think you'll find that, having had his fun, he was trying to wriggle out of marrying her. That's why she, or possibly her mother, came up with the scheme.

'One thing I don't understand is why Jason took it so quietly.'

'Perhaps he was afraid of his uncle getting to know? From what he told me, Philip Lorne has always been very strait-laced.'

'Far from being strait-laced, Lorne has got his nephew out of quite a few scrapes in the past,' Gray said positively. 'So many in fact that he'd put his foot down and told Jason that if he got into any further trouble, his allowance would be stopped.

'It's ironic really that for once in his life Jason took the threat seriously. If he *had* told his uncle, I've no doubt Lorne would have helped him.'

'But what could he have done?'

'What he's done in the past when other women who were after Jason's money tried to trick him into marriage—paid her off.'

Paid her off…

But this time the woman in question was her stepsister. It was her own family Gray was taking about with such critical contempt.

Seeing her stricken face, he said, 'I'm sorry if that sounds brutal.'

Through a dry throat, she asked, 'What makes you so sure she was only after his money?'

'Oh, come on!'

'Have you ever thought that she might genuinely love him?'

Gray's white teeth flashed in a mirthless smile. 'It's my bet that she loves his money a lot more.'

'You're seriously warped,' Rebecca accused, her voice hoarse. 'You presumed *I* only wanted to marry him for his money.'

'At first, knowing how things stood, it seemed more than likely.'

'You mean I was part of the clan.'

'At the time I thought so. Can you blame me?'

'So to prove that I was just out for all I could get, you offered me a free holiday.'

'It wasn't like that at all.'

'Then why did you ask me to come with you?'

'Because I wanted your company.'

'The company of someone whose family you talk about so contemptuously?'

'You know perfectly well that isn't how I feel about you.'

'I don't know anything of the kind.'

'What can I say to ease your mind?'

'You could admit you might be wrong about Lisa.'

'Do you genuinely believe I am?' he challenged.

She wanted to say yes, but couldn't.

'No, I thought not. At least you're honest.'

'That's a laugh!' she cried bitterly. 'I just wish to God I'd had the sense to stay in London.'

'I'm sorry you feel like that, because—'

The heat of futile anger rising inside her, without waiting to hear any more, she scrambled to her feet and fled.

When she reached their bedroom it was pleasantly cool and dim. At the half-open window the muslin curtains billowed slightly in the night breeze.

Sinking down on the bed, she covered her face with trembling hands. If only she had never agreed to come to California, never been stupid enough to let herself be drawn into this ill-judged affair...

It would have been bad enough if they had been merely holiday companions. Being lovers made things so much worse.

But she didn't *have* to sleep with him. He had offered her a room of her own, so she would *have* one and take care to keep her distance.

She rose to her feet and switched on the light. Then, opening her wardrobe, she began to bundle her things together.

'Leave them,' Gray said.

Turning her head, she saw he was standing in the doorway, watching her. His dark face serious, he added, 'I'll move out, if you want me to.'

'Yes, I do.' Close to tears, she hurried into the bathroom and bolted the door behind her.

When she emerged some ten minutes later the room was empty and his clothes had gone.

After tossing and turning until the early hours of the morning, she finally dropped off to sleep, but it was a restless sleep that brought unhappy dreams, and she awoke with tears on her cheeks.

The room was full of light and heat, and there wasn't a breath of air. The curtains hung limply at the windows, while reflected sunbeams shimmered on the white ceiling.

For a moment or two she couldn't think where she was, then it all came flooding back. The drive to Napa, their arrival at Santa Rosa, Gray so unexpectedly acting the fool, his ardent lovemaking, the shared meal and, just when everything seemed so wonderful and romantic, their quarrel.

If it could be called a quarrel.

Rather, it had been understanding, for the first time, how Gray really felt. She had been shocked and saddened by the way he had sneered at romance, and his obvious contempt for her family.

But if it was true that Lisa had lied to get Jason to marry her, and she felt oddly sure that it was, perhaps she couldn't blame him for thinking so badly of them all.

And no matter what he said about *not* including her, he must firmly believe they were all tarred with the same brush. It was obvious that he hadn't invited her because he liked her, or for her company, as he'd said, but simply to fulfil a sexual need.

With a heavy heart she wished yet again that she hadn't been foolish enough to get involved with him.

However, she had, and now it was too late. She was stuck here with no means of getting back, which meant a fortnight spent in his company.

Shuddering at the thought, she wondered just how bad it would be. But that, of course, would depend on his reaction to what had happened. She still didn't know him well enough to be able to predict which way he'd jump.

Would he sulk? Be angry and vindictive? Try to get her to change her mind about sleeping with him, and make her life a misery when she didn't? Or would he be cold and distant?

The latter would be by far the easiest to cope with, and she could only hope he'd play it like that. If he was prepared to go his own way and let her go hers, they needn't see too much of each other.

On the other hand, if he chose to be really difficult and obnoxious, he could make the coming two weeks unbearable.

Pushing the far from pleasant thought away, she looked at her watch. It was almost lunchtime. He was bound to be up by now. So what should she do?

Common sense told her there was little choice. She couldn't stay in her room indefinitely, so she might as well go out and face him, see what kind of devil she had to cope with.

Just the previous day her heart would have leapt at the thought of seeing him, but now it lay unmoved. It seemed that the powerful sexual attraction she'd felt was over as quickly as it had begun.

When she had showered, deciding it was too hot to wear a bra, she pulled on a pair of briefs and a loose cotton shift that tied on the shoulders. Then, fastening her hair into a single thick plait, she took a deep breath and followed the aroma of fresh coffee through to the kitchen.

Looking fresh and vital in stone-coloured jeans and a dark blue T-shirt, a tea towel draped around his lean hips, Gray was standing at one of the work surfaces, breaking eggs into a bowl and beating them.

His manner was relaxed, almost laid-back, and no horns were visible.

Glancing up at her approach, he said equably, 'Good morning. I hope you slept well?'

Taken aback by his friendly tone, it was a moment or two before she lied, 'Very well, thank you.'

Pouring the eggs into a pan and beginning to draw them into the centre, he told her, 'I was just about to give you a call. I thought we might have lunch by the pool. Omelette and salad suit you?'

So he'd decided to act as though nothing had happened. It was the one thing she hadn't thought of, but, willing to follow his lead and keep things on a civil footing, she answered politely, 'Yes, fine, thank you.'

'I do like a woman who's easy to please.'

If there was a *double entendre* there she let it go. Adding the large, golden omelette to a trolley containing a green salad, a crusty loaf, some smooth curls of butter, a bowl of oranges and a pot of coffee, he whipped off the tea towel and invited, 'Lead on, MacFerris.'

Without thinking, she asked, 'Shouldn't that be "Lay on"?'

Striking an attitude, he declaimed, 'Methinks that Shakespeare is oft misquoted.'

Only the previous day she would have laughed. As it was, his clowning failed to amuse her, and, barely managing a smile, she led the way out to the pool.

It was a lovely morning, the sun high over the eastern rim of the valley, and the bees busy amongst the flowers.

They sat in the shade of a fringed umbrella and ate in

what might, to an onlooker, have been mistaken for a comfortable silence.

In truth it was an uncomfortable one, on Rebecca's side at least, and she tried hard to think of something to say.

But, inhibited by the knowledge of how he felt about her, she could think of nothing. All the pleasure had gone out of being with him, and she would much sooner have been left alone.

She was aware that Gray looked at her from time to time, as though trying to correctly judge what her mood was, but, apparently wary of putting a foot wrong, he let the silence reign.

After a while, relaxing her guard a little, she found her gaze straying in his direction. He was peeling an orange, the rind sliding in an unbroken coil through his lean brown hands.

As he pulled the flesh into segments he glanced up and, seeing she was watching him, offered her a piece.

She shook her head mutely and looked away.

When they had done eating and finished drinking their second cup of coffee, he suggested casually, 'I thought we might take a look at the winery, if you're still interested?'

She toyed briefly with the idea of refusing, of quietly making it clear that she no longer wanted his company. But it might mean the onset of fresh hostilities, and she didn't want to risk that.

'Yes… Yes, I am,' she said at last.

'But you were thinking of saying no?'

She met his enquiring glance with a guilty one of her own.

'There's no need to answer, I can see you were.

'Look, I'm sorry you were so upset last night. It must have been very unpleasant to hear your family criticised in that way.

'But if you want me to retract what I said about your

stepsister, I'm afraid I can't. I believe it's the truth, and I'm sure you do.

'I'm convinced that both she and her mother are quite unscrupulous and will use any dirty trick in the book to get what they want.

'That doesn't mean I think *you* are like that. In fact I'm certain you're not. I firmly believe that you've been the innocent victim in all this.

'Jason, on the other hand, is very much to blame. If he was more discerning and less licentious, he would save everyone, including himself, a great deal of trouble.'

Gray finished speaking and waited for Rebecca to say something. When she didn't, he sighed. 'I had hoped speaking out would clear the air, and that we could get back to where we were.'

She looked at him, her face stony. If he thought that an apology and a facile assurance that he didn't include *her* in his condemnation would put everything right, he was very much mistaken.

'But it seems I was wrong…'

When she still said nothing, his manner becoming coolly brisk and determined, he said, 'So what if we go take a look at the winery?'

CHAPTER EIGHT

RISING to his feet, he held out his hand, an unmistakable challenge in his green eyes.

Unwilling to engage in open warfare, she reluctantly put her hand in his and allowed him to pull her to her feet.

When she would have freed it, however, his grip tightened just enough to make it clear that he had no intention of letting it go.

Realising with a sinking heart that she was now facing a war of attrition, she gave in and, feeling rather like a prisoner, allowed herself to be escorted down the steps and into the garden.

The cloudless sky was the colour of lapis lazuli and the Californian sun poured down golden as honey. Beyond the circle of lawns and flowerbeds, as far as the eye could see, were row upon row of vines, green and lush, climbing the hillside in orderly ranks.

A crop-spraying helicopter clattered noisily along the valley, flying low over the vineyards, a trail of spray suspended behind it like fine mist.

Reaching the low wall that separated the garden from the rest of the property, they went down another flight of steps to the large stone building that housed the wine-making plant.

Ranged alongside were some enormous hoppers, and several enclosed conveyor belts. Noting her interest, Gray explained, 'They would have been used to carry the grapes from the harvesting lorries into the winery itself.'

Ignoring the big main doors, with their rusting locks and peeling green paint, he led her around the building to a side-door.

'This looks to be a better bet.'

Releasing her hand, he took a bunch of keys from his pocket and selected one.

It turned at the first attempt.

'More by good luck than good management,' he admitted with a grin as he pushed open the door to the accompaniment of creaking hinges.

Disused for a number of years, the winery stood empty apart from its existing plant, and the confines of the long, hangar-like building echoed to the sound of the heavy door swinging shut behind them, and their footsteps.

Not much light filtered through the high, dusty windows, and in the warm, musty dimness they walked until they reached a series of prefabricated buildings that Rebecca took to be offices.

A desk and chair, and a couple of old filing cabinets, proved her to be right on the first.

Opening the door of the second, Gray said, 'This is obviously the computer room, where all the information about every single vintage will have been stored. It's also where the machinery that controls the temperature of the fermentation vats is overseen.

'Then next door, I think you'll find, is the lab where, when we get into production, our chemist will do his stuff...'

Carrying on until they reached a flight of stone steps, they went down to the vaulted fermentation chambers that held the huge stainless-steel vats, with their various dials and levers.

Down here, Rebecca found, it was appreciably cooler, even dimmer, and oddly scary, like the setting for some horror movie.

'It all seems very dead at present, even a touch sinister,' Gray remarked, echoing her uneasy thought. 'But it'll come to life again when all these vats are full of wine and the dials are winking.'

She had no doubt he was correct, but right now, oppressed by the atmosphere, she couldn't wait to be outside in the sun again.

Perhaps that sense of urgency came through, because without another word Gray began to lead the way back to the stairs.

Hurrying after him, in her haste she caught the toe of her sandal against the rough edge of a flagstone and tripped.

Quick as a flash he turned and fielded her, taking her weight against his chest.

The breath momentarily knocked out of her, she lay against him, while all the attraction she had told herself was gone for good came flooding back.

But she mustn't allow herself to be attracted.

Regaining her balance, she attempted to pull free, but his arms closed around her, holding her there.

In a sudden panic, she braced her hands against his chest, and tried to push him away.

She might as well have tried to move a monolith.

Staring at the strong column of his throat, she ordered jerkily, 'Let me go.'

'Afraid to look at me?'

Lifting her chin, she met his eyes. 'No, I'm not.'

'Good.'

Before she could guess his intention, he bent his head to cover her mouth with his.

She began to struggle, but, pinning her arms to her sides, he held her easily while he kissed her long and leisurely.

When he finally drew back a little, she cried hoarsely, 'You're nothing but a brute. I hate you.'

His mouth swooped once more and, taking advantage of her parted lips, he deepened the kiss, exploring her mouth with a kind of insolent enjoyment that set every nerve in her body quivering.

It was punishment, she knew, but even so, her senses

reeling, she wanted to put her arms around his neck and kiss him back.

When he finally released her, dizzy and off balance, she staggered and he was forced to reach out and steady her.

'All right?' he queried after a moment.

Refusing to answer, she gathered the shreds of her dignity around her, and headed somewhat drunkenly for the stairs.

Walking beside her, he put a strong hand beneath her elbow.

She was mortified to find she was glad of it.

They were almost at the end of the winery, when Gray paused briefly to take a closer look at one of the pieces of equipment.

Anxious to get outside, Rebecca carried on and reached the door first. Noticing he had left the bunch of keys dangling in the lock, obeying a sudden wild impulse, she slammed the door and locked it.

Let him stew in his own juice for a while, she thought with a surge of heady triumph.

A moment later, the keys in her hand, she was hurrying away.

By the time she reached the house the feeling of triumph had started to fade, and apprehension was fast taking its place.

Her legs suddenly shaky and a hollow sensation in the pit of her stomach, she dropped the keys on the patio table, and sank into the nearest chair.

Why in heaven's name had she been so idiotic? she berated herself. He would be furious.

Still, after the way he had treated her, he deserved all he got.

But two wrongs didn't make a right, conscience pointed out, so it was no use attempting to justify her actions. It had been utterly stupid, and would do nothing to help the situation.

Already feeling bad, she felt even worse when she contemplated the fact that sooner or later she would have to let him out and face his wrath.

She had no doubt that the longer she was doing just that, the angrier he'd be. Perhaps if she went straight back now and apologised?

To hell with that! her fighting spirit answered. She might as well be hung for a sheep as a lamb. But, agitated and restless as she was, with nothing to do to pass the time, every minute was going to seem like an hour…

'Cooee!' a voice called. 'Anyone at home?'

A second or two later Gloria Redford appeared round the side of the house. She was wearing blue cotton trousers, a tie-dyed top and the same old sneakers.

'Hi!' she said cheerfully. 'I'm just off to Napa, so I thought I'd pop in to see if there was anything you needed. Mr Gallagher's working, I suppose?'

Without waiting for an answer, she carried on, 'You're not looking too happy… If you're feeling bored, do you want to have a run into town with me?'

To Rebecca the offer seemed to be the answer to her prayers. Carefully, she asked, 'How long are you likely to be there?'

'No more than an hour.'

'Well, if you're sure it's no trouble?'

'None at all. I'd appreciate the company.'

Rebecca hesitated for a moment, wrestling with her conscience. But Gray wouldn't come to any harm, and she'd let him out the moment she got back…

'In that case I'd love to come. I'll just get my bag and lock the door.'

'Do you need to lock up, if Mr Gallagher's home?'

'He's in the winery,' Rebecca said and, feeling her face grow hot, turned and hurried into the house to find her bag.

While the older woman did her shopping, Rebecca strolled around the pleasant town. Any other time she would have really enjoyed seeing Napa, but today it was simply a distraction, and her heart wasn't in it.

When the best part of an hour had passed, having agreed on one of the coffee shops as a meeting place, Rebecca found a table and sipped a cappuccino while she waited.

Gloria arrived some twenty minutes later. Saying shopping always made her hungry, she ordered a large coffee and a plate of cookies.

A good-natured, garrulous woman, when she found Rebecca had little to say she launched into an account of her family while she worked her way through the cookies.

She had, she announced with no trace of self-pity, three young sons, a husband—who was a labourer in the wine industry—an arthritic mother and her elderly father-in-law to look after. All of whom lived under the same roof.

'We could really do with a bigger house, but through no fault of his own Ben has just lost his job, so we'll be lucky to keep this one.

'Unless your Mr Gallagher would be willing to put in a good word for him? I mean, when the company starts re-staffing the Santa Rosa winery?'

'I'm afraid I can't answer that. But you could always try asking him,' Rebecca suggested.

'Thanks, I will. Ben's very experienced—he's done everything from picking to driving a lorry and working in the fermentation rooms.'

After a while, growing restive, Rebecca glanced furtively at her watch, and was horrified to see how quickly the time had flown by. 'I really ought to be getting back,' she said, and waved for the bill.

'That's fine by me,' Gloria agreed accommodatingly. 'Though I'll have to stop for gas first.'

By the time Rebecca had climbed out of the battered pick-up at the entrance to Santa Rosa, more than three hours had elapsed.

Gray was bound to be hot and thirsty, she thought anxiously, and no doubt he'd be absolutely *livid*. Her imagination provided her with a picture of him pacing like a caged tiger.

Oh, if only she'd had more sense. But it was much too late for regrets.

She thanked Gloria and, panic snapping at her heels, practically ran up the drive. By the time she reached the house she was hot and perspiring freely, and her hands were so unsteady it took several attempts before she could unlock the door.

Having finally managed to let herself in, she went straight through and opened the sliding glass panels that led onto the patio.

The bunch of keys had been lying in the sun, and the hot metal almost burnt her hand as she snatched them up and hurried towards the winery.

Her heart pounding, her breath coming uncomfortably fast, she found the right key after a couple of attempts, and, unlocking the door, pushed it open.

Apart from the creaking of the hinges, there wasn't a sound. Holding the heavy door, she looked along the length of the building. There was no sign of movement, and not a soul to be seen.

Reluctant to venture any further, she stood in the doorway and called his name.

When there was no answer, she called again several times, as loudly as possible, and stood listening to the echoes.

Perhaps he was in the office, or the lab, or the computer room? Thinking about it, Gray wasn't the sort of man to do nothing while he waited. He would almost certainly be using his enforced imprisonment to think and plan for when Santa Rosa became fully operational again.

She knew from her earlier visit that the door closed itself, but, unable to find a way to prop it open, she was forced to let it bang behind her.

Making her way down to the prefabricated buildings, she peered through each of their windows in turn.

All three were undoubtedly empty.

Her heart throwing itself against her ribcage, she thought, what if something had happened to him?

But what could possibly have happened to him?

Suppose he'd been going down to the fermentation chamber? He might have tripped on the stone steps and banged his head. He could be lying seriously injured, or even dead.

Oh, dear God, and it would be *her* fault.

Her footsteps loud in the silence, she forced herself to go to where she could see down the steps. There was no sprawling figure.

Well, he had to be *somewhere*.

The only place left where he could possibly be was the fermentation chamber itself. Advancing to the top of the steps, she called his name.

There wasn't a sound.

But he *must* be there.

She called again, despairingly.

Only silence greeted her.

Gritting her teeth, she marched down the steps and peered into the gloom.

It seemed to be deserted.

Dreading the thought of going any further into that eerie place, she turned to go back.

Then, knowing she couldn't just walk away without checking properly, she forced herself to walk the length of the chamber, peering to right and left as she went.

When she reached the end, she realised she'd been holding her breath and let it out in a long, shuddering sigh.

It just didn't make sense.

Unless he was playing some cruel game of hide-and-seek to get his own back?

Suppose he was lurking behind one of the vats, waiting to spring out on her? Or maybe creep up silently behind her?

Fighting down her over-active imagination, she told herself sharply not to be a fool. Apart from anything else, in such a vast, empty, echoing space, the lightest brush of a foot against the stone floor would make a noise she was bound to hear.

All the same, she couldn't prevent herself from hurrying and keeping glancing over her shoulder.

It was a great relief when she reached the stairs, and by the time she had climbed them her legs were starting to feel like chewed string.

She was almost at the end of the winery when a dark shape huddled beneath a wooden rack full of dusty bits and pieces caught her eye. The hairs prickling on the back of her neck, she forced herself to walk over and take a closer look.

It seemed to be a pile of old sacks. Stooping, she picked up the top one to make sure there was nothing underneath, and dropped it again hastily when a large spider ran out.

Backing away and straightening up unwarily, she found her hair was caught on a series of hooks that dangled from beneath the rack. In a sudden panic, she tried to pull free.

Realising it was only making matters worse, she forced herself to stand quietly for a few seconds before putting up her hands to feel for the hooks. By the time she managed to free the last strand, her hair had come unplaited, she was covered in dust, and half suffocated.

Hurrying to the door, she dragged it open and almost fell out into the fresh air and sunshine. Then, leaning against the wall, she took several deep breaths while the tension that had gripped her eased a little.

When she felt a bit better she re-locked the door and made her way back through the garden, wondering all the time where on earth Gray could have got to.

But one thing was certain, he couldn't have vanished into thin air, so somehow he must have found a way out of the place…

Busy with her thoughts, she had reached the pool before she realised that he was in the water, moving in a smooth, effortless crawl. His clothes had been tossed over one of the loungers.

She felt a rush of mingled emotions. Relief that he was quite safe, futile anger that she'd put herself through so much torment, and a mounting fear that soon she would have to answer for what she had done.

In the middle of a racing turn at the far end of the pool, he saw her. Levering himself out of the water in a single, lithe movement, he began to walk towards her.

Stark naked, with an all-over tan and the physique of an athlete, he looked superbly fit and virile, and she caught her breath.

His eyes never leaving her face, he advanced so purposefully that it took every ounce of courage not to turn and run.

It wasn't until he got closer that she noticed his shoulder was bruised and he had a nasty-looking cut on his upper arm.

Taking the bunch of keys from her hand, he tossed them onto one of the pool-side loungers, and, surveying her dusty, dishevelled state, enquired silkily, 'Enjoyed your second tour of the winery?'

His manner was quiet, almost pleasant, but beneath that calm veneer she could sense he was furious.

When apprehension kept her silent, he pursued, 'You've been a long time.'

'How do you…?'

'I was on my way down the hillside, after taking a look at the vines, and I watched you go in.'

Her jaw dropped. 'Why didn't you call out to me?'

'Why do you think?'

Watching her confusion, he said, 'When you left the keys in the lock, I was sorely tempted to get a bit of my own back.'

She shuddered, and, her mouth dry, asked, 'How did you get out?'

'Through one of the windows.'

'I thought they were too high.'

'So did I, until I eventually managed to find the remains of an old metal ladder.'

Seeing her gaze was fixed on the jagged cut on his upper arm, he added, 'It gave way just as I got the window open.'

'I—I'm sorry,' she stammered.

'I'm glad to hear it.'

'Not for locking you in.' The rebellious words were out before she could prevent them.

He raised a dark brow.

'If you hadn't kissed me like that... But I didn't want you to get hurt.'

'It's only a scratch,' he said dismissively.

But it was a lot worse than that, and she asked anxiously, 'Did you put some antiseptic on it?'

'No.'

'You should have done.'

'I couldn't get into the house.'

Watching her hand fly to her mouth, he said wryly, 'When I found everything locked up, I thought you might be anticipating a siege.'

'I went into Napa with Mrs Redford,' she admitted in a small voice.

'Yes, I saw the pick-up bring you back. Three hours is a long time to be left cooling one's heels.'

Biting her lip, she stayed silent.

'But no doubt you thought I deserved it. That it was fitting retribution.'

So far he hadn't so much as raised his voice, but he wasn't the kind of man to allow a woman to get the better of him, and she wondered when he would finally unleash his pent-up anger.

The waiting, in itself, was a form of punishment, building up the tension, fraying her nerves until they threatened to snap.

Longing to sit down and have a cool drink, she wiped a trickle of perspiration from her grimy forehead with the back of her hand.

'You look all hot and bothered,' he commented, moving towards her. 'Perhaps a swim might help?'

There was a hint of smooth menace in his voice that rattled her further, and, retreating a step, she shook her head. 'No, I don't—'

Still advancing, he urged, 'I can thoroughly recommend it. But you wouldn't want to go in with your clothes on, would you?'

In a single swift movement, he caught the hem of her dress and pulled it over her head.

She wasn't wearing a bra, and in spite of her protests it was the work of a moment to strip off her dainty briefs.

'That's better,' he said approvingly.

'Leave me alone,' she cried, backing away. 'I don't want to go in. I can't—'

The words ended in a strangled yelp and a splash, as she tumbled backwards into the deep end.

She came up gasping and choking, helplessly thrashing the water, before going under again.

A moment later, from behind, strong hands caught her under the arms, and with one swift kick Gray carried them both to the surface.

Held safely by him, she filled her lungs with air, and her first wild terror began to subside a little. Still she felt panicky, her breasts rising and falling with her laboured breathing.

'You're quite safe,' he assured her. 'I won't let you go.'

Turning onto his back, so that his body supported hers,

he settled her head on his chest and smoothed the long strands of wet hair away from her face.

After a minute or so, reassured by his strength and confidence, she began to relax and they floated easily together.

Feeling that change, he said quietly, 'Forgive me, I had no idea you couldn't swim.'

'When I was quite small I fell into one of the local ponds and almost drowned. It frightened me half to death, so I never did learn.'

'Don't you think it's time we remedied that?'

'It may be too late.'

'It's never too late. The first step is to stop being afraid, and learn to enjoy the water. Are you happy at the moment?'

'Yes,' she admitted.

The water was pleasantly warm. She could feel the brush of his taut thighs against hers, and the way the slight motion of his arms made little eddies.

Perhaps it was her reaction to being safe, but her limbs felt heavy and languid, and she was filled with an unaccountable happiness.

After a while, he said softly, 'Stretched out like this, anyone can float. Give it a try.'

A moment later she was floating without his help, just his hand cupping her head lightly, reassuringly. As he'd promised, the water supported her, bore her up, and with a feeling of gladness, of release, she let go of her fear.

Even when he removed his hand, it didn't return.

'Kick down,' he instructed.

She obeyed, and they were face to face, his hands circling her waist.

Looking down at her, he asked softly, 'Did I ever tell you how beautiful your breasts are?'

Her cheeks grew hot as she remembered her nakedness, but the expression on his face made her want to glory in it, rather than try to hide it.

As though sensing how she felt, he cupped the nape of

her neck with one hand, and used the other to lift her face to his.

That gentle touch was command enough, and her lips parted in response.

While he kissed her deeply, into the vacuum left by the ebb of her previous fear a different sensation started to flow, a passionate need that came in liquid waves, sweeping over her, drowning everything in its path.

Responding to that need, he slid both hands down her neck and shoulders, then, one hand spread across the small of her back, he brought the other up under her breasts.

She made a little sound deep in her throat as he caressed the wet, smooth skin and found the sensitive nipples, which firmed instantly beneath his touch.

Then, with a shudder, she closed her eyes and gave herself up to the sheer pleasure his skilful fingers were evoking.

When both his arms slid around her, drawing her against him, she went willingly, pressing even closer until her nipples were brushing the sprinkle of crisp dark hair on his chest.

'Put your arms around my neck,' he whispered against her lips, 'and we'll share a new experience.' When, feeling his hard male need of her, she obeyed, he cradled the backs of her thighs and guided them into place around his waist.

Her desire as strong as his own, she locked herself there, her long hair floating around their shoulders like mermaid's tresses.

His arms holding her, his legs moving just enough to keep them afloat, he made love to her with tenderness and passion, filling her being with such intense delight that she gave a little gasping cry at each long, slow thrust.

His eyes gleaming with a purely male triumph, he encouraged her, 'Yes, my love… Yes…' until she cried out one last time and began to shudder helplessly against him.

When she became conscious once more of the water lapping around her shoulders and the warmth of the sun on her head, her inhibitions returning, she started to pull away.

'Don't,' he said urgently. 'I realise you're used to bottling up your emotions, hiding what you're thinking and feeling, but don't do that with me. Talk to me.

'You enjoyed what we just shared, didn't you?'

She nodded.

'Not good enough, I'm afraid. I want to hear you say it aloud. I want you to *tell* me what you were thinking and feeling.'

But she had stopped thinking, and she could find no words to express such extremes of feeling.

Looking up at him, she whispered, 'It was absolutely wonderful.'

'Is that all?' he teased.

Lifting her chin, she added wonderingly, 'I never knew physical pleasure could be so...*intense*...'

He kissed her gently. 'Some of it was due to the fact that you were so terrified previously. Extremes of sensation heighten one another.

'Now, feeling confident enough to make it to the side on your own?'

'I don't think so,' she admitted.

'Then come here.' Settling her cheek against his shoulder, he lay on his back once more, and paddled them lazily to the shallow end.

As soon as she found her feet he hauled himself out and, water pouring off him, turned to offer her his hands. A moment later she was standing dripping beside him.

His eyes running over her appreciatively, he bent to lick a drop of water from one of her pink nipples, before drawing it into his mouth.

The desire she had thought appeased came back with a rush, but, uneasy in the broad daylight, she gasped, 'Don't! Someone may see us.'

'Mmm...' he murmured, and continued to suckle with obvious enjoyment.

Her instinct was to hold his dark head to her breast, but, refusing to give way to it, she took a handful of wet hair, and tugged.

He retaliated, and, feeling the light pressure of his teeth, she let go of his hair and froze.

When, in his own good time, he released her and drew back, she turned and bolted into the house.

Gathering up her clothing and his own, he followed at a more leisurely pace.

Still partially entangled in a web of sensual pleasure, Rebecca had showered, shampooed her hair and was blow-drying it before it came home to her exactly how idiotic she had been.

With no intention of resuming their affair, she had done just that.

No, she hadn't, she corrected herself quickly. Certainly she'd behaved stupidly, but just because she had let him make love to her again, it didn't mean she was prepared to go on with the affair.

But it *did* mean that she was going to find it harder to convince him she really meant it when next time she said no.

Well, she would just have to make her position clear straight away, so he knew the score.

But she didn't relish the prospect.

If only she'd behaved more sensibly in the first place it wouldn't have been necessary. If she hadn't locked him in the winery, she wouldn't have ended up in the pool...

Still, some good had come of it. Apart from all the pleasure they had shared—which she didn't want to think about—he seemed to have forgotten his anger, and she had undoubtedly taken the first big step towards conquering her fear of water.

She finished drying her hair, and, wrapping herself in a

bathsheet, opened the door a crack and peeped into the bedroom.

When there was no sign of Gray, she went through to find some clothes.

Pulling on a cotton shirtwaister, and leaving her hair loose around her shoulders, she went outside. As she had expected, he was lounging on the patio. There was a tray of drinks at his elbow.

He looked coolly elegant in pale trousers and an olive-green shirt open at the neck. Rising to his feet at her approach, he settled her into a chair, enquiring, 'Are you getting hungry?'

'Not really.'

'Then I'll leave it a little while before I rustle up something to eat. In the meantime...' He poured two tall glasses of Pimm's, and handed her one.

'Thank you.' She drank thirstily.

When her glass was empty, taking a deep breath, she began, 'About what happened in the pool. I didn't mean to—'

'Behave so wantonly?' he mocked her gently.

Watching her cheeks grow warm, he said with satisfaction, 'You're beginning to lose some of those built-in inhibitions, and let go—'

'But that's just it,' she broke in desperately. 'I shouldn't have done. I didn't want to—'

'You'd be happier if all our lovemaking took place in bed at night, behind closed doors?'

'No, that's not what I mean. I don't intend there to *be* any more lovemaking. I didn't mean to go on with this...affair... I didn't *want* to...'

Immediately the air was thick with tension.

Stammering a little, her golden eyes pleading, she went on, 'W-we're in separate rooms now and I'd like it to stay that way.'

'I see,' he said slowly. 'So you still haven't forgiven me for what I said about your family?'

The noise of a motorbike coming up the drive practically drowned out his words. Almost immediately the engine note died, and they heard the faint peal of the front doorbell.

'It seems we have a visitor. Excuse me.' He rose to his feet and disappeared into the house.

CHAPTER NINE

REBECCA sighed. The interruption was more than welcome. Having made her point, she didn't want to get involved in another diatribe on her family's lack of principles.

Gray had been gone only a short time when the motorbike engine spluttered into life once more and was vigorously revved up. A moment later it roared away down the drive.

Whoever it was hadn't stayed long. Perhaps it had been Mrs Redford's eldest boy bringing a message?

As though to confirm that, Gray reappeared with an opened envelope in his hand. His face giving no clue to what he was thinking, he tossed it on the table and resumed his seat.

Then, as though waiting for some question, he slanted her a glance. When she said nothing, he asked casually, 'Fancy going out?'

'Going out?'

'Having failed to reach us by phone, your admirer has sent a hand-delivered invitation to a barbecue party this evening.'

'My admirer? I don't know what you mean.'

'Andrew Scrivener.'

'Andrew Scrivener?'

'If you go on like this we shall have to change your name to Polly.'

She took a deep breath. 'Andrew Scrivener has invited us to a barbecue party this evening?'

'Got it.'

When she still looked blank, Gray said, 'If you remember, the night we had dinner in Boston he told us that he was coming out to California, and that he owned Hillsden

151

Wineries. Hillsden is only about eighteen miles away, which, as he observed, makes us practically neighbours.'

'Now you mention it, yes, I do remember. But it had gone clean out of my head.' Apologetically, she added, 'So much happened later…'

His smile slyly reminiscent, he murmured, 'Yes.'

Feeling her face grow warm, she objected, 'But didn't he say in a week or so?'

'That's what he said.'

'So presumably he's brought his visit forward for some reason.'

'Exactly.'

He put so much meaning into the word that she lifted her chin abruptly. 'You don't seriously think *I'm* the reason?'

'I don't doubt it. I saw the way he kept eyeing you that night in Boston. Like a cat looking at a saucer of cream.'

'Oh,' she said blankly.

'So you'd better get your best bib and tucker on.'

'Then you intend to go?'

'Unless you don't want to.'

She didn't but, unwilling to say so out of hand, she asked, 'Will it make any difference to your business deal?'

'I very much doubt it. So feel free to say so if you don't want to go.'

He had said a *barbecue party*… Wondering if some different company might ease the current situation between them, she hesitated.

Noting that hesitation, he gave her a challenging smile. 'On the other hand, if you want to make hay while the sun shines?'

Stung by his words, his inference that she wasn't so different from her family after all, she picked up the gauntlet and, returning his smile with a brilliant one of her own, agreed, 'I might just do that. What time do we need to start?'

Perhaps, even then, she was hoping he would back down, say he hadn't meant it, that it had been merely a joke.

But, his face devoid of expression, he said, 'Half an hour should do it.'

'Then I'll go and find my best bib and tucker.'

Her heart like lead, she left him sitting there and went back to her bedroom.

As a gesture of defiance she made up with care, before brushing out her hair and swirling it into a smooth coil on top of her head. Then, donning a silky, slim-fitting sheath in navy-blue, she slid her feet into dull-gold sandals and fastened gold hoops to her neat lobes.

She had just emerged when Gray appeared, and, noticing that he hadn't changed, she wondered if she was over-dressed for a barbecue. Well, if she was, she would just have to brazen it out.

He looked her over from head to foot, and, vexed by that arrogant appraisal, she twirled to give him a back view.

'Perfect,' he approved. 'Just the right combination of sex-iness and classiness to get Scrivener going.'

'I'm so pleased you think so.'

They walked out to the car in the golden light of a late evening. There was no sign of a breeze and the air seemed to be holding its breath.

'Do you want the top up or down? In other words, are you afraid of getting ruffled?' Gray asked, mockery in his voice.

'Down, please,' she said crisply.

With music playing softly, and the gentle flow of balmy air like velvet as it caressed her face, she should have en-joyed the drive.

But she didn't.

His dark face set, his manner withdrawn, as though deep in thought, Gray drove in silence and without a single glance in her direction.

Daylight was giving way to dusk when they drew into the driveway of Hillsden Wineries, and as they neared the sprawling ranch-style house they saw that the place was ablaze with lights.

To the right, a gravel parking area already boasted a string of prestigious cars.

Drawing up alongside them, Gray commented sardonically, 'This should give you a good idea of the company Scrivener attracts. Not an ordinary wagon in sight.

'By the way, before we go in, may I give you a word of warning? If you're not serious about becoming the fourth Mrs Scrivener, don't let him get you alone.'

'And if I am?'

'Do the same as you did with Jason—play hard to get. He'll respect you for that.'

She hadn't played hard to get with *him*, she thought, feeling a kind of despair. With Gray, there had never been any hesitation. Instinct alone had ruled her...

He slipped from behind the wheel and, with his usual courtesy, came round to cup her bare elbow and help her alight.

All the windows in the house had been thrown wide, and as they approached they could hear the sound of music and laughter. The music, she noted, was smooth and middle-of-the-road.

A moment later Andrew Scrivener stepped onto the porch and lifted a hand in greeting.

'Our host appears to have been looking out for us,' Gray murmured in Rebecca's ear. 'Just shows how keen he is.'

As if to confirm this, Scrivener came down the steps to meet them.

His heavy face, and the grizzled, crinkly hair brushed straight back from his forehead, were tolerably familiar. But this time, dressed informally in lightweight fawn trousers and a white open-necked shirt, he looked younger than she recalled, and somewhat less intimidating.

Even so, that powerful face, with its large, hooked nose and sensual mouth, sent a shiver down her spine.

'Gallagher… How are you? Nice to see you again.' He clapped Gray on the shoulder with a surprising show of bonhomie.

'Miss Ferris…' His hooded eyes lingering on her face, he lifted her hand to his lips in a gesture that, on a lesser man, might have appeared overdone. 'I'm pleased you could come.'

A glint in his eye, Gray said, 'Rebecca wouldn't have missed it for the world, would you, darling?'

Scrivener glanced at him sharply, before turning to escort them inside.

The large room, and the terrace beyond, seemed to be full of people standing in little groups, laughing and talking, all with glasses in their hands.

Along with their designer party clothes and Californian tans, they sported the unmistakable aura that success and money brought in their wake. Yet there was an atmosphere of informal friendliness that was very pleasant and welcoming.

A stunning blonde, dressed in gold harem trousers and a bra-top, detached herself from the crowd and, making a bee-line for Gray, took his arm.

'Hi! You must be Gray Gallagher. I'm Sue Collins, Jeff's sister, and the unofficial hostess.

'First of all, there's a senator here dying to meet you! Then I'll get you a drink and introduce you to the rest of the crowd.'

A second later, in one of the neatest manoeuvres Rebecca had ever witnessed, Gray was whisked away.

Finding herself left with Andrew Scrivener, she said the first thing that came into her head. 'I didn't realise you were travelling to the west coast quite so soon.'

Those obsidian eyes, set deep beneath almost black brows, looked straight into hers. 'Some business I considered urgent came up,' he said smoothly, 'so I changed my plans and flew in yesterday.'

Flustered by their almost hypnotic quality, she dragged her gaze away and, indicating the party going on around them, asked, 'How on earth did you manage to arrange all this in so short a time?'

'My manager, Jeff Collins, said if I didn't mind the whole thing being simple and informal, he and his sister would make all the arrangements, and he would do the barbecuing. So I left them to it.

'Now, how about a drink?'

Already regretting coming, she answered, 'Yes, please, I'd love one.'

Spreading a hand across the small of her back in what could only be described as a proprietary manner, he ushered her through the open French windows and onto the terrace.

An almost full moon, silver and ethereal-looking, was rising above the trees, and the air was fragrant with the scent of flowering shrubs and woodsmoke from the big barbecue.

A couple of well-stocked trestle tables covered with white cloths made up the bar, while a little way away two more stood empty, waiting for the food.

As her host had said, it was all quite informal, and guests drifted up to help themselves to whatever drink they fancied. Most of them, she noticed, were choosing wine.

'Now then, what would you like, Rebecca? I may call you Rebecca?'

Forcing a smile, she replied politely, 'Of course,' just as Gray, with Sue Collins in close pursuit, appeared by their sides.

Ignoring them, Scrivener said, 'And do call me Andrew. So what's it to be?'

About to say lemonade, she changed her mind. 'I'll have a glass of wine, if I may, please…'

'Andrew…' Scrivener prompted.

'Andrew,' she echoed obediently, avoiding Gray's mocking eyes.

'I can recommend the Cabernet Sauvignon,' he told her and proceeded to fill two glasses.

Gray chose a non-alcoholic drink on the grounds that he was driving, and then, accompanied by Scrivener and Sue Collins, they began to circulate.

As though to make his intentions abundantly clear, Scrivener always managed to put his bulk between Rebecca and Gray, and while he introduced her to a variety of people he curved his hand around her slim waist and left it there.

Though she was made uncomfortable by such close proximity, his touch was so light and easy that she could find no valid reason to object.

Deciding to ignore it as best she could, she did her utmost to concentrate on the interesting people she was meeting.

Though a lot of the guests were in the wine trade as growers or shippers, mingled with them was a world-famous author, the US senator that Sue Collins had mentioned earlier, and an ex-president.

There was also, causing a flutter of excitement among the ladies, a Hollywood director and a handsome male star, who were filming in the area.

Occasionally, caught up in separate conversations, the pairs moved from group to group at different times. But, despite all Sue Collins' efforts, Gray never left Rebecca's side for long, while Scrivener never left it at all.

Only when the ex-president came up and murmured, 'I'd like a word in your ear, Andrew,' did he reluctantly excuse himself and move away.

'Judging by our Andrew's manner,' Gray said in an undertone, 'you're home and dry...'

His cynical words hurt, and she bit her lip as he went on, 'I feel I ought to offer my congratulations, but I see my watchdog homing in.'

Almost as tall as he was, and curvaceous to the point where her bosom appeared to be inadequately restrained by the low-cut bra-top she was wearing, Sue Collins slipped a hand through his arm, and pressed herself against him.

'I need a big, strong man.' She fluttered her eyelashes at him. Getting no response, she pursued, 'Jeff's busy at the moment, so will you be a sweetie and bring up some more wine for me?'

'Certainly.' Gray gave Rebecca a droll look and allowed himself to be led away.

A moment later there was the dull boom of a gong being struck, and a shout of, 'Come and get it!'

Huge oval platters piled with steaks and chicken, sausages and ribs, corn on the cob and vegetable brochettes appeared on the empty tables along with rolls, various salads, plates, cutlery and napkins.

The guests milled about, helping themselves to food and topping up their drinks. Then while some stood around in little groups eating and talking, others sat on various chairs and loungers, or perched on the low wall surrounding the terrace.

Seeing Andrew Scrivener coming back, Rebecca glanced around anxiously. She could see no sign of Gray, and though she hated his cynicism she wanted him there as protection.

Looking pleased to see her alone, Scrivener said, 'I'm sorry to have had to leave you, my dear.'

She found her voice and assured him, 'That's quite all right.'

'Now, suppose we get something to eat while it's good and hot? What would you like?'

When he had filled two plates with chicken and salad, and refilled their glasses, indicating a table and two chairs set beneath one of the old cedar trees, he suggested, 'Let's get away from the crowd.'

Remembering Gray's warning, she hesitated. Had this been planned?

But they wouldn't be *alone*, she reassured herself, they

weren't that far away from the house, and there were plenty of people within sight.

All the same, she followed reluctantly as he led the way down the terrace steps and across the smooth green lawn.

As he pulled out a chair for her, she felt a cowardly urge to turn and run. But she was just being foolish, she told herself sternly, sitting down. If he showed any signs of doing anything she objected to, she could simply get up and walk away.

In the event, he behaved like a perfect gentleman, and while they ate, at his most charismatic, he talked easily about music and a series of symphony concerts he'd been to.

Deciding that, no doubt influenced by Gray, she must have been imagining some ulterior motive, she relaxed somewhat.

Even so, not wholly comfortable, she was wondering how soon she could suggest that they rejoin the others, when he queried casually, 'Do you like the Napa Valley?'

'Very much, what little I've seen of it.'

He nodded his approval. 'The west-coast climate suits me and, as I've every intention of living out here for at least part of the year, I'm having a house built.'

She could vaguely recall that the night they had dined together in Boston he'd mentioned it.

'Close to here?' she asked, for something to say.

'Just the other side of the garden, where the hill starts to climb. It's as good as finished, and they'll be starting on the pool next week. Come and take a look. I'd like to know what you think.'

Getting to his feet, he added with rather touching pride, 'I drew up the plans myself.'

Reluctant to appear churlish, she rose.

Even then, if he had touched her in any way, she would have made some excuse not to go, but he merely waited for her, smiling.

He was a big man, as tall as Gray, and heavily built. Very aware of his bulk looming by her side, she accompanied him along an unpaved path that skirted the garden.

It was a bright, moonlit night, the air still and balmy, the sky a deep, cloudless blue pricked with stars. A beautiful night for romance.

Only Gray didn't believe in romance.

She wondered what he and Sue Collins were doing, then wished she hadn't as a picture of the blonde's ample cleavage flashed into her mind.

'How is the holiday going?' Andrew Scrivener's voice broke into her thoughts.

'Very well,' she answered evenly.

After a moment, he went on, 'When we met in Boston you said you were still carrying a torch for young Beaumont, and the relationship between you and Gallagher was quite platonic.'

When she said nothing, he went on, 'I thought he might have managed to change your mind.'

Carefully avoiding his eyes, she asked, 'What makes you think that?'

'Two reasons. Where before you were merely beautiful, now you look alive…glowing…'

'I can explain that,' she said lightly. 'I've started to catch the sun.'

'I didn't mean that kind of glow. You look fulfilled. Like a woman who's quite recently been made love to. Can you explain that?'

For one mad moment she considered telling him the truth, but even to end his pursuit—if that was what it was—she couldn't bring herself to admit she'd been such a fool.

Shaking her head, she suggested, 'Perhaps you've had too many glasses of wine?' Then hastily, 'But you said *two* reasons.'

'Gallagher's Cerberus act.'

'I beg your pardon?'

'The way he's been guarding you. He's scarcely left your side, and when he has he's never taken his eyes off you. He appears to be as jealous as hell.'

'He certainly has no reason to be,' she said with perfect truth.

'I'm delighted to hear it.'

There was so much satisfaction in his voice that she felt a quiver of alarm.

They were quite a way from the house now and there wasn't a soul in sight. She could still hear the music faintly, but it only served to make her feel even more isolated.

Wishing she had had more sense than to come, she began a shade desperately, 'It's further than I expected. If Gray's waiting to go home, he'll wonder where I've got to.'

Scrivener laughed. 'If I know Sue Collins, he'll have his hands full. In any case we're almost there. You'll see it any second.'

They reached a gap in the trees, and there it was in front of them, a sprawling, split-level place built into the hillside.

For some reason she had expected it to be soulless and ultra-modern, all sharp angles and straight lines. Instead it was colour-washed and harmonious, with long, arched windows and a covered balcony that gave it a charming old-fashioned look.

Though the moonlight leached away the colours, leaving everything an eerie silvery blue, she could tell that in daylight it would be quite vibrant.

'Why, it's lovely!' she exclaimed, momentarily forgetting her apprehension.

He looked pleased by her enthusiasm. 'I'm glad you like it. Let me show you the inside.'

'No!' Then more moderately, 'No, thank you. Some other time perhaps.' *In broad daylight with at least one other person present.* 'Gray didn't want to be too late starting back,' she lied.

'Very well,' he gave in gracefully. 'Some other time. But

I'd like you to see it. I think you'll be impressed. It has some unusual features.'

'And you were able to design it all yourself?'

'When I was young, I trained as an architect. I wanted to create something lasting and beautiful.'

Seeing a sensitive side that she hadn't realised existed, for the first time she found something to like about him.

'Now it's merely a hobby I enjoy, along with music. Of course, I still have what amounts to a passion for beautiful things. Especially women.

'Though it takes more than mere beauty to touch my heart these days. I've had three wives, all of them beautiful, all of them with brains, but somehow it hasn't worked.

'None of them have had the qualities I've been hoping to find in a woman.'

Wary of the turn the conversation was taking, Rebecca began to walk determinedly back the way they had come, and of necessity Scrivener followed her.

'As well as being sexually attractive,' he pursued, 'I want my next wife to be honest, to have strength of character and a maternal streak, as well as a certain *je ne sais quoi* that sets her apart from other women.'

As they reached the edge of the trees he stopped abruptly and, gripping her upper arms, turned her to face him.

'After we met in London all those months ago, I found myself thinking about you, unable to get you out of my mind. I was convinced that, as well as brains and beauty, you had almost everything I'd ever wanted in a woman.

'I learnt as much as I could about your background and family life, and I was about to try to arrange another meeting, when I heard a whisper that you were engaged to young Beaumont... It was something of a blow.

'Seeing you again in Boston was not only a surprise but also a great pleasure, and when you said you would like children it confirmed my earlier impression that you're just the woman I've been looking for.

'I'm not a young man any longer and I can't afford to let the grass grow under my feet, so I'm taking this opportunity to ask you to marry me, Rebecca.'

Though she had been apprehensive, half waiting for something to happen, now it *had*, she was stunned and speechless, totally unprepared.

As she stood as though turned to ivory in the moonlight his grip tightened and, drawing her close, he bent to kiss her.

Coming to life, she cried, 'No, don't!'

His hold slackened a little, and she pulled away as far as his grip on her upper arms would allow. 'I can't marry you. I don't love you.'

'I don't expect you to love me,' he said decisively. 'I'm well aware that you're still carrying a torch for young Beaumont, but now he's no longer on the scene to complicate matters—'

'I could never marry a man I didn't love,' she burst out agitatedly.

'It doesn't matter a great deal whether you love me or not, so long as you make me the kind of wife I need. In return I'll give you everything you could possibly want. I'm good in bed, I can keep you happy and satisfied, take the best care of our children...'

As she began to shake her head, he went on, 'I'm a very rich man. I can provide the kind of lifestyle some women would kill for—'

'I don't want to marry you,' she broke in urgently, 'and I certainly don't want your money.'

'Don't you want what it could buy? Think! If you had unlimited money, what would you choose? Diamonds? Pearls? Mink? A yacht?'

'I don't want any of those,' she cried hoarsely.

His black eyes on her face, he persisted, 'There must be something you've dreamt of owning? Something you'd give your eye-teeth for?'

'Only one thing… Elmslee Manor. My family home.'

'Is it on the market?'

'It was.'

'Then consider it yours. I'll give you the deeds on the day you marry me.'

'You don't know what you're saying. It would cost a small fortune.'

'I have a large fortune. If it happens to be already sold I'll offer the buyer more. Double if necessary. Everyone has a price.'

Looking him straight in the eye, she said clearly, '*I* don't.'

His grip tightened and he dragged her against his big, heavy body, crushing her to him. 'Damn it, Rebecca, don't play games with me. You're what I want, and I intend to have you.'

'No! Let me go!'

But, holding her easily in spite of her struggles, he gripped her chin with a powerful hand and an instant later his hot, wet mouth was covering hers, the fierceness of his kiss stopping her breath and forcing her head back.

It was her worst nightmare come true.

Then suddenly he was plucked away from her as though he was a lightweight and sent staggering backwards. 'Perhaps you didn't hear the lady say no?' Gray's voice, though quiet, was full of menace.

Regaining his balance, Scrivener snarled, 'What the hell has it to do with you?'

'Rebecca happens to be my guest,' Gray said, putting an arm around her waist, 'and as such I feel responsible for her.'

'She's not a child.'

'As I don't have you down as a child molester, she'd no doubt be safer if she was.'

'Damn it, man, I wasn't molesting her. I've just asked her to marry me.'

'Yes, I heard. I also heard her refuse.'

'She may change her mind.'

'I very much doubt it.'

Rebecca had stood mute and frozen, listening to the two men, then all at once, reaction setting in, a wave of nausea washed over her and she began to tremble violently.

In response to that involuntary movement, Gray's arm tightened and he glanced down at her ashen face. 'We'd better get you straight home.'

Turning to the other man, he said coolly, 'Goodnight and thanks for the party.'

They were moving away when he added over his shoulder, 'Oh, by the way, Sue Collins seems to be looking for a rich husband. She's just assured me she would do *anything* for a man who could give her the kind of lifestyle she's set her heart on.'

Sketching a mocking salute, Gray led Rebecca across the garden to where his car was parked and, her knees feeling like jelly, she sank into it with relief.

He drove back to Santa Rosa without saying a word, while Rebecca shrank into herself, her mind refusing to let go of what had happened that evening.

As her skin crawled and nausea filled her, time and time again she unwillingly relived the moment when Andrew Scrivener had crushed her to him, and his mouth, with those thick, sensual lips had closed over hers.

As soon as they came to a halt by the veranda, before Gray could come round and help her, she stumbled out of the car, and the instant he had opened the front door of the house she made to brush past him.

He caught hold of her arm. 'Where are you off to in such a hurry?'

She turned large, unseeing eyes on him. 'I'd like to take a shower.'

His face softened. 'Very well. Don't be long, and I'll fix us a nightcap.'

Going straight to her bathroom, she stripped off her

things, stepped into the shower stall and for a long time stood under the flow of hot water, letting it run over her face and into her mouth, trying to wash away any last traces of that kiss.

A loud rap at the door made her jump. 'All right in there?' Gray called.

'Yes,' she answered in a muffled voice.

'I'll give you five more minutes.'

She turned off the shower, rubbed herself dry and, pulling on a towelling robe, took the pins from her hair and brushed out the damp, tangled mass.

Then, too tired to bother getting dressed again, she slipped her feet into mules and went out onto the moonlit patio just as she was.

He settled her into a chair and passed her a brandy. As she opened her mouth to protest, he said firmly, 'It's for medicinal purposes. You need it.'

'Perhaps I do.' She took a sip, and felt its smooth, fiery warmth slide down her throat to banish the last of the lingering nausea.

His eyes gleaming silver in the moonlight, he studied her face. 'Feeling somewhat better?'

She nodded.

'I'm sorry you had such an unpleasant experience.'

'It was partly my own fault,' she admitted. 'I should have had more sense than to go with him.'

Then anxiously, 'What if he withdraws from the deal now he's been humiliated?'

'My guess is, he won't. He's too good a businessman to let anything get in the way of making money.'

'Suppose you're wrong?'

He lifted broad shoulders in a shrug. 'If I am, Finance International will just have to weather it.'

'I'm only sorry things happened the way they did. Perhaps if I'd behaved differently…'

'You mean, if you'd agreed to marry him?' Gray asked with grim humour.

'It's no laughing matter. You may find yourself in serious trouble with Philip Lorne, and it will be all my fault for behaving so stupidly.'

'There's no need to start blaming yourself. If it hadn't been for you, Scrivener would have already pulled out.'

'I just wish you hadn't had to get involved,' she said miserably, 'then at least he couldn't have blamed *you*.'

Gray gave her an ironic smile. 'Are you suggesting that instead of riding up on my white charger I should have left you to defend your own honour?'

Repressing a shudder, she assured him, 'I'm very pleased you didn't.' Then guiltily, 'And I haven't even thanked you yet.'

'Think nothing of it. Any time you need rescuing just let me know and I'll make sure I'm on the spot.'

That sparked off a thought, and she asked curiously, 'How come you *were* on the spot? How did you know where to find me?'

'When I'd looked all over for you, I did what I should have had the sense to do in the first place; put pressure on Sue Collins.

'She admitted that the whole thing had been arranged, and that when she had got me safely out of the way Scrivener was planning to show you the house he's having built.

'I was hoping against hope that you wouldn't be fool enough to go inside, and it was a great relief when I reached the trees and saw the pair of you start to return.

'Everything seemed to be fine, so I decided that, rather than make an uncomfortable threesome, I would stay out of sight until you'd passed, and then cut across the garden back to the house.

'Fortunately, as it turned out, I found myself unwittingly

eavesdropping when you stopped fairly close to where I was standing.'

'But if you overheard everything, why didn't you…?' With a sudden unhappy realisation of what his answer would be, she faltered to a stop.

'Step in sooner? I can only apologise for not doing so. But I still wasn't one hundred per cent sure that you weren't playing hard to get, that you didn't *want* to be the fourth Mrs Scrivener.'

'So you *did* think I was just like the others…' she whispered, her hurt showing.

He shook his head. 'I didn't think that. I've never thought it since first meeting you. Though I must admit a few doubts had crept in.

'On the first occasion this marriage thing came up you didn't exactly dismiss it out of hand. In fact, if I remember rightly, you said something like, "I'll bear that in mind."

'And tonight, when I mentioned making hay while the sun shone, you answered, "I might just do that."'

'I only said those things because I was hurt by your attitude and what *you'd* said. I had no intention of doing anything of the kind.'

'Then why did you choose to go to Hillsden?'

'I didn't *want* to go, but I thought a party might help to ease the…the situation…'

'If only I'd realised that. But when I discovered you'd gone off with Scrivener quite happily in spite of my warning, it made me wary of interfering.

'Though I couldn't resist following to make sure you were all right.'

In a heartfelt voice, she said, 'I can only thank God you did.'

CHAPTER TEN

AFTER a moment, his voice thoughtful, Gray said, 'I must admit that I was fascinated to learn what lengths he'd go to to try and persuade you.

'Knowing how much you love Elmslee Manor, I did wonder if offering you that might do the trick.'

Rebecca shook her head. 'Though I'd give the world to have Elmslee, I'd never marry Andrew Scrivener to get it.'

Jokingly, he asked, 'If *I* happened to be rich enough to offer you Elmslee, would you marry me?'

'No,' she answered unhesitatingly. And knew, even as she spoke, that if he wanted her for his wife she would marry him if he hadn't got a penny and could offer her nothing but a shack.

'So you put me in the same class as Scrivener?'

'You must know perfectly well I don't.'

'Then it's because you still love Jason?'

'I don't still love Jason,' she said flatly. 'I realised that the morning we left Boston.'

'If that's the case, as you've been willing to sleep with me, I'm intrigued to know why you wouldn't marry me if I was rich enough to give you Elmslee as a wedding present.'

'Because you'd always believe you'd bought me.'

'And you'd like your husband to respect you?'

She lifted her chin. 'Yes, I would.'

'Fair enough... But there's one important thing you haven't mentioned.'

When she just looked at him, he said, 'Love. I heard you tell Scrivener that you could never marry a man you didn't love.'

'No, I couldn't.'

'And of course you don't love me.' It was a statement not a question. All the same he seemed to be waiting for an answer.

About to assure him she didn't, she paused, knowing it was a lie. From the moment he had walked into the summer house she had been lost. In Boston she had warned herself not to let him become part of her life, *necessary* to her, but it had already been too late. She had loved him even then.

But she mustn't admit it. He'd made it plain that he didn't want any emotional entanglements, and if he learnt the truth now it would only embarrass him...

'Having trouble deciding?' he queried.

'N-no...'

'No, you're not having trouble deciding? Or no, you don't love me?'

'No, I don't love you.' Despite all her efforts her voice shook slightly.

'But what guarantee is there that love will make a marriage work? It would have been a terrible mistake to marry Jason.'

'Yes, I know,' she admitted quietly. 'Though, looking back, I can see now that I never really did love Jason. It was just infatuation.'

Sighing, she added, 'I suppose, never having been in love before, I couldn't tell the difference.'

They both fell silent, and after a moment, watching her stifle a yawn, Gray said abruptly, 'Time for bed, I think.'

All at once her breathing grew shallow and her pulses quickened. Now he was finally convinced that she wasn't a gold-digger, if he suggested moving back into her room she would welcome him with open arms.

But he made no such suggestion.

When they reached her bedroom door, he hesitated for a moment as though about to kiss her goodnight. Her lips had parted in eager anticipation, when he walked away with just a quiet, 'Sleep well.'

Sleep, however, proved to be elusive, and she tossed and turned restlessly for what seemed an age. When she did finally drop off, it was to dream that she was trapped in an underground maze with no way out, and Andrew Scrivener close at her heels.

He reached out of the darkness to grab hold of her and she awoke with a silent scream, drenched in perspiration and with a wildly beating heart.

Afraid to go back to sleep again, she lay with her eyes wide open, staring up at a ceiling dappled with moon shadows.

She wanted to be with Gray, wanted the comfort of his arms and the feel of his body next to hers. Wanted to lie with the man she loved.

But perhaps he no longer wanted her?

No, she couldn't believe that. Some instinct told her that, while he didn't love her, he *did* want her. So why hadn't he suggested moving back?

The answer came immediately. Because he was too proud. His leaving had been at her behest, so he was waiting for her to ask him to come back.

Or go to him.

He might be asleep, the hesitant part suggested.

If he was, which somehow she doubted, she could always wake him.

But after what she had said earlier in the evening, it would mean sinking her pride.

So what? Pride was a cold bedfellow. And after this holiday he would go back to the States and all she would have would be memories.

Barefoot, and in her thin cotton nightie, she padded to his door and knocked.

After a moment it opened, and he stood there naked.

Taking a deep breath, she said awkwardly, 'I seem to be making a habit of this.'

'I'm certainly not complaining.' Smiling at her, he added, 'Though you are a shade overdressed.'

The rest of the holiday proved to be sheer bliss and they enjoyed life to the full. Some days they took the car and went sightseeing, either inland or to the coast; others they walked hand in hand or just lazed in the sun.

Gray taught her how to swim with some degree of confidence, and even dive, and, having come across a pack of cards, she taught him how to play cribbage, a game she had often played with her father.

At times they shared a companionable silence, at others they talked freely, but by tacit consent they avoided all personal topics. They ate simply, and mostly out of doors, except for in the mornings, when, having made sweet love for most of the night, they breakfasted in bed before showering together.

It was the happiest time Rebecca had ever known and she wanted it never to end.

Then all too soon the last morning arrived, and with it Gloria Redford, who had popped in to return their clean laundry and resume her caretaking duties.

For once she said hardly anything, apparently made speechless by the huge tip Gray gave her, and the promise that he would do his best to find a job for her husband without delay.

Touched by his kindness, and battling against the feeling of sadness that the end of the idyll brought, Rebecca felt tears sting behind her eyes. But somehow she managed to keep smiling while they said their goodbyes, and set off to drive back to San Francisco. They were boarding the plane before she thought to ask, 'Will we be going straight through?'

'No, as it's such a long haul I thought it best to break

our journey in Boston, so I've booked a room at a hotel near the airport.'

Rebecca sighed. In less than twenty-four hours they would be home and parting company. But, as though they were both determined not to spoil their last day together, neither of them mentioned it.

When they reached London it was damp and overcast, and the contrast to the golden days they had just spent lowered her spirits even more.

As soon as the airport formalities were over, a uniformed chauffeur appeared as if by magic to deal with their luggage and lead them to where a sleek limousine was waiting for them.

As he began to load their cases into the boot, she braced herself and said to Gray, 'If it's out of your way to drop me, I can always get a taxi.'

'It isn't out of my way,' he answered evenly.

Handing her into the car, he followed her in and took a seat beside her, before adding, 'Though unless you insist, I wasn't intending to take you home just yet. There are still a lot of things to be settled.'

Her heart gave a little flip. 'Things?' she echoed.

He looked at her with those fascinating green eyes. 'I presume you won't be taking up Scrivener's offer of a job?'

'No, I certainly won't.'

'Then we still have your future to consider. I thought, if you're agreeable, you could stay at my house until we've had a chance to really talk?'

It was a wonderful, unexpected gift, and, choked by excitement, all she could do was nod.

'Good,' he said casually. 'Then we'll discuss the various possibilities as soon as I've dealt with the business that brought me back to London.'

*   *   *

The white-stuccoed town house they drew up in front of had a handsome portico, long windows and a basement guarded by black wrought-iron railings.

Situated in a quiet square near Regent's Park, it was much bigger and grander than anything she might have imagined.

While the chauffeur dealt with the luggage, Gray explained, 'It was my grandparents' house. Jason always referred to it as "the family mausoleum".'

'Why was that?'

'Come and meet the housekeeper, and you'll no doubt understand why. Mrs Sheldon is somewhere in her nineties. She's been with the family since the year dot, and she still runs the household with the proverbial rod of iron.

'I offered to have a stairlift installed, but she soon put me in my place. She said *when* she was too old to climb the stairs she would let me know.'

Grinning, he added, 'She called me *Master* Graydon until I was twenty. I'm quite fond of her. She's one of the reasons I keep the house on. I think it would kill her if she had to leave.'

Opening the door, he ushered Rebecca into a large wood-panelled hall with an elegant staircase and a crystal chandelier.

As he closed the door behind them a small, upright figure appeared, dressed neatly in black. Her silver hair was taken up in a bun, and the skin of her pale face stretched so tightly over the bones that it appeared translucent.

She could well have been a corpse, Rebecca reflected, if it hadn't been for the small, birdlike eyes that were so amazingly alive and intelligent.

'Mr Graydon. It's nice to have you back.'

'Thank you, Mrs Sheldon.'

'Did you have a good holiday?'

'Marvellous.' Gray put an arm around Rebecca's waist, and smiled at her.

Her heart in her eyes, she smiled back.

'Mrs Sheldon, this is Miss Ferris.'

'How do you do?' Rebecca turned to the old lady, whose sharp gaze had been assessing her.

After a moment, with what seemed to be a nod of approval, the housekeeper said, 'If you'd like to freshen up, Miss Ferris, I'll show you to your room.'

So Gray had made arrangements for her to stay before he'd even asked her!

As she glanced at him, he said easily, 'When you come down again you'll find me in the den.'

Mrs Sheldon, proving more sprightly than Rebecca would have expected, led the way upstairs and opened a door to the right. 'This is the Rose Room. I hope you'll be comfortable.'

'Thank you. I'm sure I will.'

'I'll get Watkins to bring up your luggage. If you need anything, just ring for Mary.'

Large and airy, the room had Regency wallpaper, a pale carpet and long windows that overlooked a walled garden. It smelled pleasantly of beeswax and lavender, and was furnished with antiques that wore the patina of age.

The first door she tried refused to open, the second led into an *en suite* bathroom that had all the trappings of the twenty-first century. It looked so inviting that she decided to have a quick shower before going down again.

There was a tap at the door, and the chauffeur carried in her case and put it on a low chest. When she thanked him with a smile, looking gratified, he gave her a smart salute.

As she opened her case and took out a change of clothing, she wondered why Gray had asked her to stay. What it was he wanted to talk about.

If it was something as impersonal as finding her a job, surely he could have given her any relative facts over the phone? She felt a heady rush of hope and excitement. Perhaps he was hoping to continue their affair?

But how could two people have an affair with the Atlantic

between them? Unless he was thinking of the odd times he came over on business?

If he was, she knew she wouldn't refuse. Seeing him, however infrequently, would be preferable to not seeing him at all…

When she had pulled on off-white trousers, a blue silky shirt and a pair of sandals, she fastened her hair into a loose knot and went downstairs.

There wasn't a soul in sight, and, having crossed the hall, she hesitated, unsure which of the several doors Gray had indicated.

She was approaching the first, which was slightly ajar, when a voice she knew, *Jason's voice,* cried in anguish, 'Oh, please, Uncle Pip, you can't do that…'

Then Gray's voice, quietly adamant, said, 'If you're going to keep behaving like a fool then I'll be forced to treat you like one.'

As she stood frozen to the spot, she heard Jason protest, 'But what the devil could I do? She assured me she was pregnant, and that mother of hers threatened to get hold of you and kick up a fuss.'

'It's a pity you didn't let her,' Gray said coldly.

'You said you'd wash your hands of me if I got into any more trouble.'

Gray sighed. 'That threat was intended as a deterrent; it wasn't meant to push you into marrying the first designing female that managed to get her claws into you.'

'I had no intention of marrying her—'

'Then why get involved?'

'It just started as a bit of fun,' Jason said sulkily. 'I'd been getting nowhere with—' He broke off abruptly.

'Rebecca?' Gray prompted.

Sounding startled, Jason asked, 'How do you know about Rebecca?'

'With so much at stake I like to keep a fatherly eye on you, so when I heard a whisper that you were seeing one of the Ferris girls, knowing how impecunious they were, I asked Billings to check.

'He sent me some nice pictures of you and a woman he named as Rebecca Ferris. Unfortunately, he failed to tell me when you decided to swop sisters.'

'I was a fool, I know, but I was hellish frustrated, and when Lisa came to my room that night... Well, she's quite something, and at first she seemed happy to keep things light.

'I can tell you it was a hell of a shock when she told me she was having a baby—'

'And you believed her?'

'Well, it was possible,' Jason admitted. 'That first night we had taken a chance...' Then angrily, 'Damn it, have you never made a mistake?'

'Yes, as you well know,' Gray said shortly. 'But I managed to learn from it. It's a pity you didn't. If you'd refused to marry her—'

'I might have done, but she wasn't just any little trollop, she was from a good family, and when she swore she was pregnant—'

'And was she?'

'While we were on honeymoon she "discovered" she wasn't. Though I was furious at the way she'd fooled me, I must admit it was a relief to know there was no baby on the way. I'm not cut out to be a father.

'I just wish I hadn't let myself be rushed into marrying the scheming little bitch.'

'If I'd found out about the wedding sooner I might have prevented it, but by the time Billings tipped me off it was too late. I can't say I was pleased that you'd gone behind my back.'

'The last ticking off you gave me you said it was time I settled down and got married.'

'I meant to a decent girl who loved you rather than your

money. Though it wouldn't be fair to any decent girl to have to put up with your lecherous ways.'

'Well, you're no saint!'

'That's quite true, but I've always stuck with one woman at a time. I suggest you do the same. Try to make something of your marriage.'

'But if you stop my allowance, how will I manage? What will I do for money?'

'Work for it. You've still got a good job with an excellent salary.'

'I'll never be able to manage on that.'

'Why not? You've no mortgage to find. The flat's paid for, though I took the precaution of keeping it in my name.'

Jason muttered something Rebecca didn't catch.

'Admittedly you won't be able to throw too much money away on other women,' Gray went on, 'and your wife will have to curtail her spending. But it should prove to be a salutary lesson. For both of you.

'After, say, a year, if you've no debts and you're still living together—and you might well be; it wouldn't be worth her while to divorce you—I'll be happy to reconsider.

'If not, I'll interpret your mother's will to the letter, and you'll never gain control of a penny.'

'Damn you, Uncle Pip, you can't do this to me. It was my father's money. I have a right to it.'

'It was not your father's money. The fortune came from your mother's side of the family. Your father was a charming but penniless ne'er-do-well when he married your mother.

'Though she was astute when it came to business, she was anything but when it came to personal relationships. She was mad about him. It took her a long time to discover that he was spending her money at a rate of knots, and mostly on other women.

'If he hadn't been killed when he was, she would have had very little left.

'That's why, knowing how like him you were, when she became terminally ill she made a will leaving everything to me, and asked me to do the best I could for you.

'Which, believe it or not, is what I've done for the past eight years and am still trying to do.

'Now, I suggest you go home to your wife and put her in the picture. If she decides to stay with you, there may yet be hope for you both...'

Wanting to hear no more, Rebecca turned and fled silently up the stairs. She had almost reached the top when Jason came rushing out. Without a glance in her direction he crossed the hall, and a second later the front door slammed behind him.

'So there you are.' Gray had followed him into the hall and was standing looking up at her. 'I was about to come up to see where you'd got to.'

Then, noting her pale face and utter stillness, 'How much did you overhear?'

'Most of it, I imagine,' she answered bitterly.

'I'm sorry you had to find out that way. I told Jason I wanted to see him in the office tomorrow, but, apparently scared by the message, he decided to call at the house to try and make his peace.'

Still scarcely able to believe it, she said, 'So *you're* Uncle Pip.'

'Yes.'

Even then she had half expected him to deny it.

'If you're Philip Lorne, why are you calling yourself Graydon Gallagher?'

'My full name is Philip Lorne Graydon Gallagher. But because I wanted some degree of anonymity, the ability to go out and about without being ''recognised'', I've always used Philip Lorne as a business name.

'It was one of the things I wanted to talk to you about. Come on down and I'll put you in the picture.'

With a feeling of utter despair, she shook her head. 'I'm going home.'

'If you still want to leave when you've heard what I have to say, I won't stop you. But first you're going to listen to me.'

When she just looked at him, her face set, he asked, 'What's it to be? Are you coming down? Or do I have to fetch you?'

She didn't doubt he meant every word, and rather than be ignominiously fetched she forced her unwilling feet to carry her down the stairs again.

When he would have put a hand at her waist, she flinched away from him. His jaw tightened and, his hand dropping to his side, he led the way back into the den.

It was a comfortable, homely room carpeted in Turkey red and lined with bookshelves. There was a desk with a swivel chair, a coffee-table and a suite in soft, natural leather. A log fire burnt cheerfully in the grate.

'Sit down,' Gray said shortly.

'I'd rather stand.'

He dropped into a chair, and, pulling her onto his lap, held her there despite her attempts to rise.

When, realising she was wasting her time, she stopped struggling, he said calmly, 'That's better.'

Sitting stiff and straight, her face averted, she demanded, 'Are you sure your wife won't walk in?'

Unruffled he said, 'Quite sure. To the best of my knowledge my ex-wife is married to an Australian businessman and living in Sydney.

'But I'd better start at the beginning. When I was born my mother was past middle age, and I already had a sixteen-year-old sister, named Anne.

'I was just a few months old when my parents were killed in a car crash and, as they hadn't altered their will to include me, Anne inherited everything.

'That didn't matter in the slightest as there was plenty of money in the family, but even so, she felt it wasn't fair.

'After the accident we came to live in this house with our paternal grandparents. They always called me Graydon, which was my grandfather's name. Only my sister ever called me Pip.

'Anne was twenty-two when she fell in love with, and married, Charles Beaumont.

'Beaumont, who was good-looking and charming and belonged to the peerage, hadn't a penny. That wouldn't have mattered at all, but unfortunately he turned out to be a wastrel and a womaniser.

'They moved into a house a few doors up from this one, and Jason was born two years later. Which made me an uncle at the tender age of eight.

'Realising that Jason was of the same mould as her late husband, when Anne found she was dying she named me as his legal guardian and gave me control of her money. I was twenty-three, to Jason's fifteen.

'Even then he was hardly ever out of trouble, and when he was barely seventeen he was expelled from boarding-school for having an affair with one of the teachers' wives.

'Rona and I had only been married a few weeks when he came to live with us. He brought a swift end to a marriage that was already doomed.

'She was very much like Lisa, beautiful, sexy, unscrupulous and from a good, but impoverished, family. Having set her sights on what she wanted, which was a rich husband, she lost no time in going to bed with me.

'She'd certainly got what it takes, and for a while I was on cloud nine. Then she told me she was pregnant, and if her mother found out she would make her have an abortion.

'We were married in the local register office as soon as it could be arranged. The day was cold and wet and the surroundings unappealing. But if the wedding was joyless, the honeymoon was even worse.

'Thinking to surprise her, I'd chosen to get away from it all in a villa in Tuscany. Rona hated everything about it—the isolation, the climate, the food—and couldn't wait to get back to London.

'Because she didn't want to live in the house my grandparents had left me, I'd bought a flat in Mayfair, and Jason came to stay with us there while I tried to find another school that would take him.

'One evening I'd arranged to work late at the office and then go on to a business dinner. At the very last minute my client rang to say he couldn't make it, so rather than have dinner alone I decided to go home.

'I got there to find the flat empty. As I was on my way to the kitchen to get a bite to eat, I noticed my study door was ajar and my small wall safe was standing open. When I checked, my grandmother's ruby ring was missing.

'Apart from being worth a great deal of money, it was a family heirloom. My intention had always been to give it to my wife, but something had held me back, and I'd bought her a diamond solitaire instead.

'I was about to call the police when I heard a sound from the master bedroom. Thinking the intruder might still be on the premises, I crept over and threw open the door.

'For days on end Rona had refused to let me touch her, saying she felt sick. Now she and Jason were in bed together, stark naked, and not only was my wife making the running, but she was also wearing my grandmother's ring.

'I lost my temper and hauled her out of bed. She'd obviously been drinking heavily; she was unsteady on her feet and she stank of gin. I called her a thief and a slut, and threatened to put her over my knee.

'She threw the ring in my face, and said if I laid as much as a finger on her she'd take me to court.

'It wasn't the threat that stopped me, but the knowledge that she was pregnant.

'When I said as much, she called me a poor sucker and

laughed in my face. She said only a fool would have fallen for that old trick.

'I spent the night in my study, and in the morning I told her to pack her bags and get out.

'Having sobered up, she tried to talk me round, but I was through. Still she proved difficult to get rid of, and in the end, because I didn't want to involve Jason, or have my dirty linen washed in public, I was forced to pay her off.'

After a moment he stroked a finger down Rebecca's cheek and asked, 'Have you listened to a word I've been saying?'

'Yes.' And it explained so much.

She turned her head to look at him, her golden eyes brimming with tears.

'Don't cry, little one.' He smiled at her with such tenderness that the tears spilt over.

'I'm sorry...' she whispered.

'For what?'

'That you've never found someone to love.'

'Oh, but I have. One day I walked into an old summer house and there was the woman of my dreams.'

'What?' She looked at him dazedly.

'The only problem is, she won't have me. I've tried to lure her with the promise of a manor house but...'

'You really would buy Elmslee?'

'The deed is done. It's signed, sealed and settled. As soon as I knew you wanted it, I contacted my agent and offered him a substantial bonus if he could push the sale through quickly.'

A thought struck her, and she said, 'I see now what you meant when you said Lisa should have set her cap at the organ-grinder.'

'Don't change the subject, woman.' He stroked a finger down her cheek caressingly. 'Now I've gone to all that trouble, won't you change your mind and agree to marry me?'

She shook her head. 'If I do, you'll believe it's only to get Elmslee.'

'That's where you're wrong. I'll believe you love me. And even if you keep saying no, I'll still believe you love me. You do, don't you?'

'Yes. But what makes you so sure?'

'When I asked you before and you said no, I watched your face. You're not a very good liar.

'Added to that, Mrs Sheldon thinks so, and she's never wrong.'

'Mrs Sheldon?'

'She's fey,' he said, as though that explained everything. 'When I mentioned I was bringing home the woman I loved and wanted to marry, she asked, "Does she love you?"'

'I told her I very much hoped so.

'She said, "I'll know for certain when I've seen the two of you together."

'When she'd shown you to your room, she came back and said very primly, "You'll be pleased to know I've put Miss Ferris in the Rose Room."'

When Rebecca looked blank, he added with a grin, 'The Rose Room is next to mine, and has a connecting door.'

Later that night as they lay in each other's arms, Gray said, 'You'll never know how jealous I was of Jason, and when Scrivener kissed you I could cheerfully have broken his neck.'

She shuddered. 'Don't remind me; it was horrible.' Lifting her face, she added, 'You'd better kiss me to take the memory away.'

'There's nothing I'd like better,' he said with satisfaction, 'especially when you think what a kiss can lead to.'

It did, and it was heavenly. Secure now in his love, she hit the heights and heard the angels singing, before floating gently back to earth.

Drawing her against him and cradling her head on his shoulder, he asked, 'How soon will you marry me?'

'Tomorrow.'

'Can't be too soon for me. But it might take a bit longer to arrange. You see, this time I want a proper wedding. I'd like us to be married in church with all the trimmings, and go on a romantic honeymoon.'

'I didn't think you believed in romance.'

'I've changed my mind... Then when we get back...' He stopped and asked seriously, 'Do you care where you live?'

'I don't care at all so long as you're there.'

That earned her a kiss. 'Well, we could spread ourselves a little. There's this place, I'm fairly certain you'll like New York, and we could go back to Napa from time to time.'

'It's going to be wonderful,' she said dreamily.

'And of course there's Elmslee, it'll be ideal for our children, and to retire to when we get old.'

She nestled even closer. 'It sounds like one of those fairy tales that end, ''And they lived happily ever after.'''

He kissed her again, and said contentedly, 'I'm quite sure we will.'

HARLEQUIN *Presents*

**She's sexy, successful
and pregnant!**

Share the surprises, emotions,
drama and suspense as our
parents-to-be come to terms
with the prospect of bringing a new life into the world.
All will discover that the business of making babies
brings with it the most special joy of all....

THE SICILIAN'S
DEFIANT MISTRESS
by Jane Porter

Tycoon Maximos Borsellino made a deal with Cass for
sex. Now that Cass wants more from him, he ends the
affair. Cass is heartbroken—worse, she
discovers she's pregnant....

On sale this February.

HARLEQUIN®
Presents

The world's bestselling romance series...
The series that brings you your favorite authors,
month after month:

Helen Bianchin...Emma Darcy
Lynne Graham...Penny Jordan
Miranda Lee...Sandra Marton
Anne Mather...Carole Mortimer
Susan Napier...Michelle Reid

and many more uniquely talented authors!

Wealthy, powerful, gorgeous men...
Women who have feelings just like your own...
The stories you love, set in exotic, glamorous locations...

HARLEQUIN®
Presents

Seduction and Passion Guaranteed!

HARLEQUIN *Presents*

**They're the men who have
everything—except brides....**

Wealth, power, charm—what else could a heart-stoppingly
handsome tycoon need? In the GREEK TYCOONS
miniseries you can meet gorgeous Greek
multimillionaires who are in need of wives.

Don't miss out on BABY OF SHAME...

BABY OF SHAME
by Julia James

Rhianna has struggled through poverty and illness,
dedicating herself to her son.
Now Alexis Petrakis has discovered that their
shame-filled night created a beautiful baby he's
determined to reclaim....

BABY OF SHAME on sale February 2006.

www.eHarlequin.com

HPGT0206